Bottled Spirits

& Other Dark Tales

Adrian Ludens

LVP

PUBLICATIONS

Cover Art by M Wayne Miller, Design by LVP Publications, © 2022 LVP Publications and Adrian Ludens

Reduced to Tears ©2017 (*Zippered Flesh 3*, 2017)
Amelia ©2018 (*Suspense Unimagined*, 2018)
Wish Granters ©2019 (*Terror Politico*, 2019)
A Pedestrian Encounter ©2018,(Drunken Monkeys, online, November 2018)
The Sodbuster and the Spider ©2018 (*Mindscapes Unimagined*, 2018)
Esoteric Insurance, Inc. ©2018 (co-authored with Evan Dicken, *Corporate Cthulhu*, 2018)
The Burial Shroud ©2017 (*HWA Poetry Showcase Vol. IV*, 2017)
Bottled Spirits ©2016 (*Grave Markers 3*, 2016)

Printed in the United States of America

Lycan Valley Press Publications
1625 E 72nd St STE 700 PMB 132
Tacoma, Washington 98404 United States of America

First Printing

ISBN: 978-1-64562-905-4

Dedicated to the memory of Shonna-Leigh C. Bunch.
A dear friend, deeply missed.

CONTENTS

REDUCED TO TEARS

Margo Thayer arrived home from work bubbling with good cheer. She'd spent the week working mornings at the supermarket and evenings wearing a headset at the call center. Tonight, she planned to spend a well-deserved night out on the town.

But first, the kids.

Margo found her youngest, Noah, playing video games in their apartment's living room. "Hey kiddo, how was school?" She bent and planted a kiss on his buzzed scalp.

His eyes never left the screen. "Fine." Noah's fingers flew over the controller as he guided a caped hero through a series of colorful explosions. Margo felt the corner of her mouth quirk. The extravagances of childhood, she thought.

"I'm going to have dinner with a few friends from the call center. Will you be okay here with your sister?"

Noah glanced up and gave her a look. "As long as she doesn't try to boss me around."

"She is in charge while I'm gone." Margo said. "That means if there's a fire, she has to carry you out of the blaze draped over her shoulder." Noah rolled his eyes at her strained attempt at humor.

"Otherwise, you won't even know she's here."

"Good," Noah said. His eyes remained glued to the pixilated distraction unfolding on screen. He winced as if absorbing an actual blow.

"I'll be home before midnight. Bedtime's at nine thirty. Don't forget."

Margo left her youngest and called for her daughter from the foot of the stairs. "Starla!"

"Yeah, Mom?"

"Just letting you know I'm going to heat up some green beans and mini-ravioli on the stove. I'm going out with Trudy and the girls tonight."

Starla poked her head out of her room. "'Kay."

Margo started dinner heating on the electric stove and then strode to her bedroom. From her closet, she selected her favorite Little Black Dress and open-toed black heels. She dressed and scrutinized herself in the full-length mirror affixed to the bedroom door.

Her shoes displayed her four remaining toes, fresh from a pedicure, nails painted black. Her hands matched her feet, with only thumb and forefinger remaining on each hand. Her ears protruded from the sides of her head, spectacularly prominent thanks to her shorn scalp and missing earlobes. Margo eyed the hollow of darkness lurking behind her half-closed left lid and grinned, exposing gaps left by the removal of her lateral incisors.

Watch out guys, she thought. Margo is coming to party!

She grabbed her purse and hurried toward the door.

Margo's headlamps diffused the darkness with yellowish, chicken-broth light as she pulled into her building's parking lot. She had left the bar well before closing time in a bid to avoid any sobriety checkpoints. In this, she succeeded. Now, before bed, she planned on a hot shower and a two-aspirin preemptive strike against a hangover.

A figure darted across the road in front of her car, and Margo stomped on the brake pedal. The figure, a teenage boy, glanced back at her and then ducked between vehicles and disappeared in the darkness beyond the parking lot. His expression, illuminated for a split-second, conveyed a mixture of surprise, fear, and then triumph. Margo eased her car into her assigned spot and mulled the fleeing figure over in her mind.

Something about him had repulsed her. His appearance—even in the briefest of glances—seemed to her seedy and unsavory. It was only as she inserted her key into the apartment door's front lock that the realization hit her.

The fleeing boy, though he had looked Starla's age or perhaps older, still had both eyes. They had bulged in surprise when she hit the brakes to avoid hitting him. Having the left eye removed at the age of ten was a rite of passage for all Reducers. Margo shuddered; only a deviant would refuse.

Margo thrust the door open and locked it behind her. She leaned with her back pressed against it, eye closed, panting. Her heart pounded, but why was she so worried? Just because she'd spotted an objectionable person in the neighborhood didn't mean her family was in any immediate or specific danger.

As she set her purse down on the entryway table, Noah, dressed in his pajamas, sidled into view. Noah, for whom she had grand hopes—so grand, in fact, that she had specified his middle name as "Body" on his birth certificate—stood in the hallway, a smirk twisting his mouth. The boy had a secret, one he clearly wished to impart.

Margo's heart fluttered on shaky wings while her stomach sank like a discarded cocoon. "I know something you don't know," Noah announced. But in that moment, Margo did know. She leaned against the wall, feeling ill. Margo drew in a single lungful of air and screeched her daughter's name.

Margo thought, for perhaps the hundredth time since starting work, of the boy who'd fled across the parking lot the previous night. She'd warned her daughter against dating—or even befriending—troublemakers like him. Starla seemed to go out of her way to make her worry.

With a deep sigh, Margo reached out, crab-clawed a package of steak, and swiped it over the scanner.

"Rough night?" her current customer asked.

Margo looked up in surprise, truly seeing him for the first time. He seemed close to her age. He too retained only index fingers and thumbs on both hands. His left eyelid drooped in what looked to Margo like a perpetual insouciant wink. His shaved head suited his rugged good looks. If she'd run into this guy last night, she wouldn't have been in such a rush to get home.

"My teenage daughter…" Margo muttered.

"Say no more," the man grinned. "They never want to make it easy on their parents, do they?"

Margo noticed he still had his upper left lateral incisor—that meant he was at least one year younger than she was. Margo resisted the urge to ask him to turn around and lift his shirt so she could see if he had a kidney-removal scar.

"No, they don't." She laughed. The man joined her. She finished ringing up his transaction and let her finger graze his open palm when giving him his change. The man blushed.

Margo hoped she'd see him again.

The days, ever similar, ran together.

On the afternoon of Noah's tenth birthday, Margo clocked out and hurried down the aisle to purchase a chocolate cake from the supermarket's bakery to help celebrate. She also bought balloons, a liter of soda, and a box of ice cream sandwiches. It came to more than she'd intended to spend—or could afford to spend, if truth be told—but she wanted to surprise her son. She pictured his face lighting up as he opened the car door.

Instead, when she picked him up from school, he climbed in and wilted in the passenger seat.

"What's wrong?" Margo asked. "Aren't you excited for your party?"

Noah remained silent for several blocks. At last, he exploded. "I wish we weren't so poor! Everyone is going to laugh at me."

Margo sighed. "Noah, honey, we talked about this. We'll get your eye removed as soon as we can afford it."

Noah squeezed his lids closed, perhaps staving off tears. He didn't respond, only began breathing through his nose in short, angry snuffles.

"As long as we get it removed before you turn eleven, we'll still be within the customary schedule," Margo said. She thought of Starla's would-be boyfriend and repressed a shudder. "I won't let it go longer than that, believe me."

"But my friends will make fun of me." Noah drew a deep, watery breath.

"Then they're not true friends." Margo braked as they reached a red light. "We just can't afford it right now. I'm sorry you're feeling embarrassed, but we can't just gouge your eye out with a grapefruit spoon, can we?"

Noah turned to face her, his eyes alight, beaming with hopeful excitement. She imagined him preparing for school the next morning with a bloody, seeping bandage affixed to his face.

"No, we cannot," Margo pressed. "It's not safe, it's not sanitary, and—oh, honey—you'd be in so much pain."

Noah sank back against the seat. Margo turned her attention back to the road. She made a mental note to hide the grapefruit spoons when they got home.

The next morning, Margo dropped the kids off at school before heading to her shift at the supermarket. Starla sat in the front passenger seat in cold silence, her arms folded across her chest, until they arrived at the middle school.

Margo slowed the car and spoke. "You can continue to be upset, but it won't change anything. If you live under my roof, you obey my rules. Those types of people never amount to anything but trouble, believe me." Starla jumped from the car, slammed the door, and melted into the crowd of teens.

Margo's car chewed up the blocks between the middle school and the elementary school Noah attended. He'd been silent as a shadow in the backseat. Now Margo reached out and angled her rearview mirror so she could see her son.

Fresh tears glistened on his cheeks. Yet he had not uttered a single word of complaint since his party. This realization sent a pang into Margo's heart. She eased the car to a stop at the curb.

"I'll make sure you get your procedure soon, okay kiddo?" She watched him cast a doubtful glance up at her and gave him a reassuring smile. "I just need to work some doubles and we'll schedule it during winter recess. How about that?"

Noah's grateful expression pleased her. He nodded and left the car, his backpack thumping against his spare frame as he hurried across the playground.

At the supermarket, Margo clocked in, counted her till, and began scanning groceries for an endless procession of customers.

When it came to standing in line, age determined the hierarchy. A reduced elderly person, usually installed on a throne-like motorized wheelchair as a matter of necessity, always went to the head of the line. The younger people, still raw blocks of sculptor's marble as far as society was concerned, waited their turn out of respect.

About halfway through her shift, she noticed the handsome man she'd conversed with enter the store. A thrill went through her when, his shopping completed, he chose her line over that of the other cashiers.

When the man reached her, Margo found that nervous excitement had erased any witty or flirtatious greetings from her brain. Instead, "Did you find everything?" was all she could manage.

The man smiled. "I did, but I also find that I have no desire to dine at home this evening. I feel like having dinner out." He glanced down at her fingers. When he looked up again, relief had relaxed his features. "I'm tired of dining alone."

Margo blushed. She knew what he intended to say next. She waited while he fumbled for his wallet.

"I'd be honored if you'd consider joining me for dinner," he said. He pressed a crisp white business card and his payment into her open palm.

She counted back his change, her voice shaking enough that she mentally chided herself for behaving like a love-struck schoolgirl. "I'll consider your offer. Thank you for shopping with us today."

The man nodded, hefted his grocery sacks, and smiled at her again. "I hope you'll call."

As he strode away, Margo stole a glance at the man's business card. Dr. Benjamin Graham, MD, the card read, Reduction Specialist. Below this, the name of a clinic, an address, and a phone number. He had written a second number in pen on the back of the card.

Margo knocked, waited a moment, and then entered her great-grandmother Millicent's room at the senior care facility. An array of machines chirped in the corner and privacy curtains shuttered the bed. The odor of disinfectant permeated the air.

Margo swept aside one curtain. "Hello? Great-Grandma Millie? It's Margo!"

"Hello." Millicent spoke but didn't move. "How are you, dear?"

"I'm feeling... conflicted," Margo said. "There's some drama in my life right now. I felt like I needed to talk to my oldest living relative."

"What's troubling you?"

Margo looked at the shape reclining on the bed and sighed. Through good times and bad, Margo relied on Millie for her sage counsel. "Starla, she's thirteen. So of course she's trying to date a boy who's one of those anti-reduction nuts."

"Oh dear."

"I'm sure she's just doing it to test me, but it's still frustrating. Then there's Noah, he just turned ten and wants his eye out so bad! I just don't have the money to take care of that yet and he's disappointed—"

"You've lost your focus."

"Excuse me?"

There was a momentary semi-silence, punctuated only by the sounds of the machines.

"Renew your spiritual focus and it will sustain you. Take me, for instance. Doctors removed my kidneys and I rely on dialysis for physical survival. My spleen is gone, as is my large intestine."

Margo remained silent.

"Doctors removed my uterus when the accustomed time came. I have one lung, no arms or legs, no eyes, nose, or ears. All of this and more—or should I say less?—is in keeping with my faith. Each removal, each reduction, serves as a blessed stepping stone toward my ultimate goal."

Margo nodded. "Of course."

"The fewer cumbersome organs and appendages I have, the closer I get to my Creator."

"I understand," Margo said. She looked at her great-grandmother, her truncated features and the tubes that kept her alive hid beneath repurposed cheesecloth. A log sawed in half and placed under the covers might have looked more convincingly human.

Millicent continued, apparently lost in reverie. "I underwent a total gastrectomy. The nutrition I receive goes straight from my esophagus to my small intestine. When the doctors determine how best to rid me of those—well, I've already signed on the dotted line."

Her great-grandmother hadn't possessed hands in two decades. Perhaps Millie had made a joke.

"Many years have passed since doctors removed my appendix, my tonsils, and my teeth," the old woman continued. "Of course I had them remove all of my teeth at once, rather than waste my forties going tooth by tooth. I'm looking forward to the removal of my tongue and the severing of my vocal cords on my next birthday. I'll have my eardrums punctured next year. I'm sure I'll feel at peace then."

"I'm going to do all that, too," Margo said. Her own voice sounded defensive and unconvincing.

"The less of us the better, when we each meet our Maker," the older woman said. "I think that's what the Good Book meant about 'separating the wheat from the chaff.' But Margo, dear, you're focusing on petty, everyday squabbles and emotions, instead of the big picture."

"You mean the reduced picture." Margo tried to laugh but it felt forced. Her great-grandmother was right, of course. Each

Reducer's journey walked a fine line between public and private experiences. Margo didn't think she could match Millie's spiritual zeal for reduction, but she'd certainly try.

She bid her great-grandmother goodbye and slipped from the room. She didn't dare bring up her silly crush now.

Despite her best intentions, her "silly crush" on Dr. Graham grew. She finally gave in and called to accept his offer. He took her to dinner at an intimate bistro where they dined, talked, and laughed.

"Please call me Ben," he said, after they had seated.

"I'm Margo. M-A-R-G-O. There used to be a silent T at the end but I reduced it."

Her companion burst into genuine laughter and Margo felt warmth growing in the pit of her stomach—or perhaps lower.

After dinner, Ben opened a second bottle of wine, and Margo opened up as well. She told Ben about her life, her children, scraping to make ends meet, and anything else that came to mind.

Her date absorbed it all. When Margo revealed Noah's middle name, he gasped. "Oh, Margo, that's beautiful." He never seemed disinterested or gave the impression that he felt superior to her in any way. Her inner warmth became heat.

In the end, they returned to his townhouse together. They made love for hours, exploring each other's bodies. Caressing surgery scars. Kissing appendages that would one day be sliced off and cast aside. On the agonizing path to purity, they found a brief moment of carnal bliss.

Everyday life, for a time, became a joy.

Starla's inclination toward freakish, two-eyed boyfriends proved to be a passing fancy.

Ben performed Noah's left eye removal off the books as a favor to Margo. When she thanked him, he said, "Severing the optic pathway to the intuitive side of his brain will help him immensely in life. I'm happy to help."

Thanks to Ben's generosity, Margo didn't have to work double shifts and could spend more time with her kids. In fact, the four of them spent a good deal of time together—until the day of Margo's fortieth birthday.

The kids were at school, and Margo, enjoying a day off from the supermarket, met Ben for lunch at their favorite Indian restaurant. They planned a more expansive dinner in celebration of her latest milestone.

"I thought we could go to Cristo's," Ben said. "You know, the Greek place on Lake Street? You could invite some of your work friends."

"That all sounds great, hon," Margo replied. "Listen, do you think you could get me in first thing in the morning?"

Ben's eyebrows shot up. "Get you in for what?"

"I'm turning forty, silly," Margo said. "I want my nose removed."

"Your... nose." Ben tried to smile, but it faltered.

"Of course, it's the next step in the reduction process."

"Right, right." Ben twisted his napkin.

"Is something wrong?"

"I just... I love your nose. It's adorable." He looked at her, his eye pleading. "I think it's your best feature."

"And not having it would make you love me less?" Margo didn't appreciate Ben's misguided attempts at flattery. Was he that shallow?

"No, of course not! I just—"

"You wouldn't try to interfere with my spiritual journey, would you?"

"You know I've dedicated my life to helping people reduce, Margo. I realize its importance. I even do charity work."

"Oh, so Noah's procedure was 'charity' work?"

"No!" Ben grimaced. "Don't misconstrue what I'm saying. I believe in the spiritual journey of reduction. I do. But I also love your adorable button nose! Can you blame me for wanting you to keep it for a few more months?"

She gazed at his face, studying him for any sign of an ulterior motive. Then it hit her. Where once warmth had grown within her, icy tendrils of disappointment now spread and tightened. Margo struggled to maintain her composure. She saw him all too clearly, realized the hidden meaning behind his words, and felt reduced in his eyes.

"Leave. Now. I want you out of my sight."

"You can't be serious." Ben stared at her. So did other patrons.

"I said get the hell out!" Margo screamed. She tried to cover her face with her abridged digits and began to sob. With one shallow declaration, the man she loved had reduced her to tears.

Frowning, Ben pushed back his chair and hurried out of the restaurant.

Margo called out sick from her checker shift the next morning. She was worried that Ben might try to confront her at the supermarket. She moped around the house, sipped tea between crying jags, and consigned to boxes anything that reminded her of him.

She knew she couldn't afford to skip both jobs, so after shuttling the kids home from school, Margo drove to the call center.

"Oh, honey," Trudy whispered, when Margo walked in. She set aside her headset and rose. "What's wrong?"

Margo sank into her chair. "Is it that obvious?" She glanced up at her friend. Trudy's features conveyed sincere concern.

"Stop me if I'm being a snoop," Trudy said, lowering her voice. "Your eye is bloodshot. I'd say you've been crying."

Margo sighed. "I have."

"What happened?"

"I just turned forty yesterday—but I didn't feel much like celebrating." Margo shrugged and then shook her head, as if carrying on a second, internal conversation. "My Mr. Right turned out to be a shallow creep. He told me not to have my nose removed."

"No!" Trudy's mouth fell open in shock.

"Can you believe it?" Margo put on her headset and prepared to take her first call. "We've only been dating a few months, and he already had the nerve to tell me I need to look younger."

AMELIA

Collecting bonsai consists of finding suitable bonsai material
in its original wild situation.

SEVEN DAYS BEFORE Father returned, Joe met the girl of his dreams.

He'd never dreamed of her, of course, had never even known of her existence until that day. Unlike his biblical namesake, Joseph Daniel Farr had never had a prophetic dream. In fact, as far as he knew, Joe had never dreamed in his life.

He sat in his black four-door Dodge, drumming his fingers on the steering wheel and listening to NPR, waiting for the guy in front of him to place his order. The topic of the program dealt with a man from somewhere in Africa who trained for marathons by running from something he feared. Joe missed hearing what the man feared; a piece of information crucial to his understanding of the runner's motives. In frustration, he turned the radio off.

The car in front of him finally pulled ahead and Joe rolled up to the drive-thru speaker.

"Welcome to Frank's Burgers," a feminine voice chirped.

"Order when you're ready."

Joe recited his order and eased forward, following the start-stop procession until he reached the pick-up window.

"Hello! That comes to five eighty."

Joe gaped. The woman wearing the yellow t-shirt emblazoned with the Frank's Burgers logo was, in his estimation, nothing short of gorgeous. She had striking green eyes, chestnut hair pulled back in a ponytail, and lips that curved into a tentative smile as he watched.

"Sir? Five eighty?"

Joe heard his total spoken as a question and realized he'd been staring. "Sorry," He glanced at her nametag. "...Amelia. I got distracted."

"Is something wrong?"

"No, everything's fine. Just perfect." Joe thrust two fives at the girl. Her fingertips brushed his as she took the money and a thrill of excitement raced through him.

She withdrew from the window and moved to the cash register. As she turned, Joe realized something unusual about the girl. She had no left hand.

He knew it was impolite to stare but couldn't help it. While her right hand looked normal—beautiful, even—a swollen stump comprised her left. Small pea-sized appendages that Joe surmised should have been fingers protruded at odd intervals. Her left forearm also looked shorter than he expected.

She returned to the window and counted back his change. His soft drink and straw came next. When she made eye contact with him, he felt a surge of sexual desire coursing through his body. His mind raced. He had to say something.

The girl disappeared from view. Moments later she returned with a folded white paper bag containing his food.

She held out his order with her right hand but as he took it, his eyes wandered again to her left appendage. He placed the bag on the passenger seat and turned to face her.

"I hope you don't think I'm out of line for asking you this," Joe said. "But—"

"Amelia." A gray cloud had darkened the green meadows within her eyes. She seemed resigned, maybe even crestfallen.

"I know," Joe said. "I read your name tag. You're beautiful."

"No, it's a condition called—" The girl at the window tilted her head and her mouth dropped open. "Wait. What?"

"You're beautiful. Gorgeous. I'd like to ask you out on a date."

Amelia shook her head, frowning. She reached to close the window. Joe read her thoughts.

"You don't believe me," he said. "You think I'm lying to be mean. I'm not, I swear!"

Amelia glanced at the line of vehicles waiting behind him. One customer tapped their horn, impatient. She withdrew, but handed a single napkin to Joe a moment later. "You better go," she said.

Not wanting to make her feel uncomfortable by pressing the issue, he did as she asked.

At the first red light, he glanced at the extra napkin. Butterflies took flight in his stomach, as if intending to lift him from the confines of his car.

She'd given him her number.

Some of the difficulties of collecting include finding suitable specimens and getting permission to remove them.

Six days before Father returned, Amelia picked up after the first ring.

"Hello?"

"Is this Amelia?"

"It is."

"Hi. It's Joseph Farr... from the drive-thru. You gave me your number."

"I remember. Hello."

"I hope you don't think I'm creepy for calling."

"Not at all. I hope you don't think I'm desperate for giving out my number."

"I didn't think you made a habit of it or anything."

"Well, you're right. Although, to be honest, nobody ever asks."

"I think that's crazy; you're beautiful."

"I think my arm freaks guys out."

"A tree grows the way it wants to grow."

"Excuse me?"

"Some people get all uptight about trees and bushes and branches, always pruning this or trimming that. I have a walnut tree growing in my front yard. The tree has a lot of character. I think it's my favorite part of the yard. There's this one branch that grows out sideways. It hangs out over the walk between the front door and the mailbox. Father always grumbled about it, kept threatening to cut it. I always stopped him. Who am I to arrest its growth? A tree grows the way it wants to grow."

"That's beautiful, Joseph."

"So are you. And call me Joe. I'd like to take you out some time, if that's okay with you."

"That's absolutely okay with me, Joe."

The main benefit of collecting bonsai specimens is that
collected materials can be mature.

Five days before Father returned, Joe elicited a genuine laugh from Amelia by suggesting they grab a quick bite at Frank's Burgers.

"You'll have to do better than that, Big Spender," she said.

"Do you know lots of people call it Frank's Greasy Burgers?"

Amelia burst out laughing. Joe mentally deemed it the most beautiful sound he'd ever heard.

"The people who work there call it that, too!" Amelia said, and this time Joe joined in her laughter.

He took her to a quiet little seafood place. They ate, drank, and made comfortable small talk.

During the meal, Joe noticed Amelia kept her left hand hidden in her lap. He wanted to tell her she didn't have to, but wasn't sure how to broach the subject.

After dinner, he suggested a movie. She agreed and he drove her to the multiplex where they stood on the sidewalk and studied the movie posters.

Much to Joe's delight, Amelia cast her vote for the latest super-powered extravaganza.

"I love superheroes," she said, noticing his skeptical look. "DC puts out better comics, but Marvel puts out better movies."

"I think I love you," Joe said, only half kidding.

After the movie, as he drove her home, he glanced over and cleared his throat. "Do you mind if I ask you a personal question?"

She considered, and then said, "All right."

"I'm just wondering about your name."

"My name?"

"Yeah. Didn't you tell me in the drive through that it was your 'condition' or something?"

"Yes. My arm didn't form right when I was an embryo. My condition is called amelia."

"But it's also your name."

"Right."

Joe lapsed into silence. He watched the white lines disappear as they drove along the highway back to her apartment. He wasn't sure if she was truly willing to have this conversation or not.

"That's what I don't understand. I mean, if the thing with your hand is called amelia, why did your parents name you that, too?" The words tumbled from his mouth. "It sounds like they put you in a box, you know? Like your entire identity is based around that one thing. I don't think that's fair to you."

Amelia smiled. "My mom and dad talked to me about that as soon as I was old enough to ask about it. See, they named me that because they wanted me to know I was much more than any perceived deformity, more than anything anyone could label me."

Joe nodded. "I think I get it."

"It's not like that old Johnny Cash song where the boy has the girl's name. I didn't need to be toughened up; I needed to know there was a world of possibilities for me." She turned to look out the windshield, as if reminded of her surroundings by her own words. "Amelia is the name they gave me, and I'm in control of what I do and who I am. My arm does not define me, nor will it dictate what I become. And let me tell you, Amelia Jenkins has high expectations for herself."

Joe smiled but kept silent.

"The only time I ever get self-conscious about it is if I'm around a guy who I think is super-hot."

"I love you," Joe said. This time he wasn't kidding at all.

*The grower can move an outdoor bonsai from a pot to a
training box to stimulate growth...*

Four days before Father returned, Joe invited Amelia over to his house so he could cook her dinner.

He prepared Caesar salad, fettuccine Alfredo with roasted chicken breast, and cooked buttered carrots. He splurged on a good white wine.

"Delicious," Amelia said.

Joe grinned. "Thank you."

"I've never had a man cook for me."

"I hope you enjoyed it."

"I did." Amelia tossed her napkin on her plate and stretched luxuriously.

Joe pushed back his chair. "I'm just going to clear the table."

"Do you need any help?"

"You just relax, missy. Maybe next time."

Amelia relocated to the little house's adjacent living room and sank into a couch she mentally categorized as worn but not ratty. She closed her eyes amid the soothing rattle of dishes. A few minutes later, feeling the call of nature, she rose.

She ducked her head into the dining room. "That wine went right through me. Mind if I use your bathroom?"

"Do you need any help?" Joe parroted her words from minutes before and waggled his eyebrows.

Amelia giggled. "You just relax, mister." She felt heat rising in her cheeks and added, "Maybe next time."

Satisfied by the look of saucer-eyed delight Joe gave her in response, she hurried down the hall.

Inside his bathroom, she closed and locked the door and examined herself in the mirror. Was she blushing? *Oh, you bet.* Hair and makeup were still great though. She felt pleased with her choice of attire. Amelia studied his toilet seat as she unbuttoned her jeans and slid them down to her knees; it looked like he'd just cleaned it.

She perched, fully aware of the grin that encompassed her face. *He cleaned it just to impress me.* Another followed this thought immediately. *I hope he washed his hands before starting dinner.* Amelia giggled.

By the time she'd finished washing at the sink, she'd decided to sleep with him. Maybe not that night, but soon. He was so charming, so sincere. A dream come true...

Amelia paused, looked at her reflection again. Her eyes strayed to her left arm. The old insecurities raised their ugly heads. Maybe he just felt sorry for her, or maybe this was all an elaborate prank. What if he was the type of guy who bedded anyone and everyone who let him?

Amelia glanced at the closed bathroom door. She turned the water back on and eased open the medicine cabinet, looking for condoms or any other indication that her host might only be interested in sex.

Cologne, aspirin, dental floss, and a dozen other mundane medicine cabinet items populated the shelves. She noted a trio of prescription bottles. Curious, she picked one up. She was unfamiliar with the medication; wasn't even sure she could pronounce it. She looked at each bottle in turn but gleaned no information from their names or warnings ("may cause dizziness", "take with food"). One thing was certain: he needed to make a trip to the pharmacy. He only had two pills left in each bottle.

A knock at the door startled her and she jumped.

"Everything all right in there?" Joe called.

Feeling guilty, Amelia closed the cabinet, turned off the water, and grabbed a hand towel. "Yes, be right out!"

Would he ask what had taken her so long? What if he accused her of snooping? She re-hung the towel and threw open the door.

"Sorry! I was daydreaming."

In the shadows of the hallway, Joe's face looked like a pencil sketch: creased brow, crinkled nose, and lips that were half smirk, half frown. "Daydreaming? About what?"

"Just wondering if you had protection. You know, just in case."

Joe blushed and shook his head. Amelia pressed her advantage. "No? I hope you address that oversight before our next date.

Thank you for dinner, Joe. I'd better get home."

She kissed his cheek and after a moment's consideration, gave him a second, lingering kiss on his lips. She left him standing there with a smile of idiotic bliss on his face and pants that she hoped felt too tight.

In the technique known as grafting, a root is introduced to a prepared area under the bark of the tree.

Three days before Father returned, Amelia visited again, and in Joe's darkened bedroom, two sheltered souls sacrificed their virginity to each other.

Despite their clumsiness, neither would forget that night for as long as they lived.

As she left Joe's house and walked to her car, Amelia noticed something amiss. At first, she tried telling herself it wasn't important, but her observation made her feel confused and betrayed. She returned to his stoop and rapped on the door.

Joe, still only wearing a bathrobe, appeared. He saw her and grinned. "Hey. Back so soon?"

Instead of answering, Amelia turned back to the sidewalk she'd now traversed several times and pointed. "I just noticed your walnut tree. You told me on the phone that you didn't want to cut the branch that grew over the sidewalk, but there is no branch over the sidewalk."

Joe's features darkened. He massaged his temples. When he looked up again, Amelia read his look of frustrated resignation.

"Father did that," he murmured. "Once, while I was away."

"'Father,' huh?" Amelia tried out the word, not liking how formal it sounded. "Why couldn't he just respect your wishes?"

"I don't want to talk about it."

Most bonsai need direct sunlight to thrive. It is the grower's
role to provide the correct lighting.

Two days before Father returned, Joe drove to Amelia's apartment.

They ordered Chinese take-out and watched a romantic comedy while they cuddled on her couch. Later, though she was still sore from the night before, Amelia took her lover by the hand and led him to her bed.

"This is like a dream," Joe said afterward. His face flushed and still panting, he fell back onto the empty side of the mattress.

"Does this qualify as a whirlwind romance?" Amelia snuggled against his chest as he stared up at her ceiling.

"Oh, absolutely," he said. "And we definitely make a hotter couple than those two in the movie we just watched."

Amelia giggled. "Thanks for bringing protection. I don't think our parents would be forgiving if you got me pregnant after less than a week of dating."

Amelia felt Joe's chest hitch beneath her as he stifled a laugh. "You want the truth? I went to the drug store like thirty seconds after you left that day."

Amelia lifted her head and studied his face. "Really?"

"Well... I might have taken care of some business first," he admitted. "But I went there right after."

"Some business, huh?" Amelia started to trail her stump down his chest but stopped, feeling self-conscious.

Joe darted a hand out before she could withdraw. He held her arm and looked in her eyes. "A tree grows the way it wants to grow."

She licked her lips, felt her heart racing. She let her stump glide over his stomach toward his penis. She watched it twitch and thicken in response.

Joe clasped the back of her neck and drew himself toward her.

They kissed, hard and urgent.

"Touch me," he breathed.

She did.

In a bonsai being prepared for display, each leaf or needle may be subject to decision regarding pruning or retention.

The day before Father returned, Amelia noticed Joe's bottles of prescription medication were empty.

She hadn't meant to snoop, it had just sort of happened.

He'd invited her over after work for a light late supper. He'd suggested she stay the night, promising to set his alarm early enough for her to shower and stop by her apartment for a change of clothes before work.

They polished off one bottle of wine and started another before relocating to his bedroom.

Later, as he dozed, she slipped from his bed to use the bathroom. As she finished, she noticed the toothbrush he'd bought her lying on the counter.

He'd beamed like a small child as he presented it to her, upon her arrival that evening. "For you, to keep here. I bought it when I bought the condoms."

The drug store, and his prescriptions, sprang to mind as she stood at the sink brushing her teeth.

Opening the medicine cabinet, she lifted each prescription bottle in turn and found them all empty.

Silly man, she thought. *Thinking more about me than about himself.*

She spat, rinsed, and made eye contact with herself in the mirror.

"He's worth keeping," she told her reflection. "Don't let him slip away."

She returned to the bedroom. Joe tossed and muttered in his sleep. He mumbled something unintelligible and kicked at the covers.

"Shhh, it's okay," Amelia said. She stroked his hair and tried to soothe him, but he seemed confused and out of sorts.

"Joe? Are you sick?"

He only muttered.

Her mind returned to the empty pill bottles. Should she try to call the pharmacy? Or call 911 and ask for information about his medications? Would he accuse her of mothering him? Amelia decided it would be worth the risk and began to crawl out of bed, but Joe reached out and touched her leg.

"Don't go. Just got a headache is all." His voice was husky from sleep.

"Well, maybe Nurse Amelia will just have to take care of you," she said, snuggling close. "I think you'll find yourself in good hands, figuratively speaking, of course."

Dwarfing of foliage is accomplished by partial defoliation of the plant. Not all species can survive this technique.

Amelia awoke and immediately felt her movement restricted. She tried to call out but couldn't. In fact, she could barely breathe. Though she tried, she found it impossible to move her arms. This wasn't like a nightmare, though. This felt more like sleep paralysis. Something heavy weighed on her hips and stomach, increasing her sense of claustrophobia. She tried to force her eyes open.

To her great surprise, her eyes opened easily. Her relief was short-lived: Joe knelt on her, pinning her to his bed. He had bound her arms to his bedposts with duct tape. She realized more tape covered her mouth.

She wasn't into rough sexual adventures and didn't want any

She wasn't into rough sexual adventures and didn't want any part of whatever he had planned. Amelia tried to arch her back, but Joe held the weight advantage. He shook his head and scowled in obvious disapproval. Then he reached for something beyond Amelia's line of sight.

"One thing that I cannot abide is a twisted limb." Joe's hand reappeared holding a large steel-blade handsaw. "So I'm going to prune it."

He touched the saw to her skin. Amelia's frantic kicks fell harmlessly on the mattress behind him.

The saw teeth bit into her flesh, jaggedly severing nerves in a storm of molten fury, Amelia writhed in pain. *Just survive,* she prayed. *This is not my destiny—I control that, not him. This experience will NOT define me...*

"I don't know what to do with him. He's too soft-hearted—and soft-headed." Joe's voice, gravelly and stern, grated her eardrums. "Each time I come back I find he's gotten himself into another predicament that needs my fixing." He gritted his teeth and leaned into his task.

Agony buffeted Amelia, rippled out from her growing wound in waves, as blood-slicked steel chewed into muscle and tendons. She recognized that the Joe she knew and loved had gone away. Someone else had come to the forefront.

Father had returned.

WISH GRANTERS

"COME ON GANG, HUSTLE!" Gada's father stood in their driveway and waved one arm like a traffic cop. "You'll miss your wish if we don't get moving!"

Gada let her mother steer her toward the family's maroon SUV. "Hurry, honey; you know how your father gets."

"I *am* hurrying." If her mother noted the petulance in her tone, she let it pass.

"This will be terrific," her father said as he slid behind the wheel. "Hundreds of like-minded people gathered for a common cause."

Gada heard his seat belt latch closed as she hunched her way to the rear bench seat. Her older brother, Colby, had already claimed the front bench, and despite her failing health, she knew better than to ask him to move. He still considered himself top dog. Gada dropped onto the rear bench as her mother climbed into the front passenger seat.

"Can we stop for food?" Colby asked. "I'm starving."

In the rearview mirror, Gada saw her father's eyes narrow in irritation. She was hungry, too, but felt relieved her brother had asked the question and drawn her father's ire.

"We'll hit a drive-thru on the way." He said and stabbed the key into the ignition. The SUV roared to life. "Gada, you get to pick, since it's your special day."

"Move it, move it!" Across the city, Missy's dad called up the stairs. "Time's wasting!"

"Are you sure we can't leave Robert at home?" Missy heard her mom ask. "He doesn't have to be part of this."

"Allie, for the last time, no." Sam sounded like he was talking to a puppy that had made a mess on the carpet. "Missy was selected by a classmate to be present for her wish. It would be an insult not to at least pretend to show our support."

"Missy! Robert! Let's go!" Not dad this time, but mom calling.

So, she had given in. Missy sighed and slid her feet into a pair of flip-flops. In the hall, her older brother brushed past her, preoccupied with his cell phone.

Out in the driveway, he and Missy played Rock Paper Scissors. Missy lost. She trudged with hunched shoulders to the back of the van. Robert plopped down up front, just behind their folks, and started messing with his phone again.

"You kids are in for a real treat today." Missy recognized an undercurrent of sarcasm in her dad's tone. She watched as he looked at each of them in turn in the van's rearview mirror. "You'll see how delusional most people in this town are. These 'wish granting' ceremonies can be downright creepy; so many people chanting and cheering, but they don't care about others. After this, you'll be proud to be what they call a 'bleeding heart' liberal."

Five minutes later, with Missy still pondering the elusive but somehow terrifying meaning of "bleeding-heart," their gray van merged onto the highway.

"The importance of the Wish Granter ceremonies is just as important as the Rallies and the Worship Services. Gada, I am so proud you were selected as the Kid Wisher for today's ceremony."

Gada's father had not stopped talking since they'd left their driveway. True to his word, he'd ordered lunch at a fast food drive-thru she'd picked, but he'd done all the talking there, too, ordering her a hamburger kid's meal without even asking what she wanted.

Tentacles of boredom dragged down her spirits. This felt even worse than the times her mother forced her to go with her to the fabric store. At least she always got to bring along—

"Donkey Hoaty!" Gada cried. "I left him in my room!"

"Well it's too late to go back now," her father said. "We're over halfway there."

"But, Daa-ad!" In her dismay, she added a second syllable. "He's gonna be lonely."

Colby's chuckle dripped with the special kind of derision only an older brother can muster. He could afford to laugh; he'd brought along one of his handheld video games.

"No whining, young lady," her father scolded. "I don't want to hear any more about that beat-up doll, you hear me?"

"He's not a doll, he's a stuffed donkey." Gada felt tired, hot, and near tears.

"Either way, no more whining."

Gada folded her arms and slumped against her seat. Outside their SUV, buildings seemed to march past like soldiers in a parade.

"Those lunatics have no one to blame but themselves." Missy's dad kept talking as he drove. His voice was loud and gravelly, and hard for her to ignore. "They blindly follow, shortsighted, never questioning anything."

In truth, Missy couldn't understand why her father was so intent on going to Gada's ceremony. When her classmate, who she didn't even get along with, invited Missy and her family to come, Missy's father had leapt at the chance to attend, despite his constant claims about how absurd the ceremonies were.

Missy pretended to be stretching, lifted her arms, and crossed them over her head. She pressed her upper arms against her ears. It wasn't enough to drown out her dad's never-ending speech.

She wished she had brought along her pillow, or—

"Dad!" Missy dropped her arms. "We gotta go back home!"

He broke off speaking and frowned over his shoulder at her. "What's the matter?"

"I want to bring Salvador Dolly along to keep me company."

Her dad rolled his eyes and turned his attention back to the highway.

"Salva-*tore* Dolly, more like," Robert scoffed. He swiped a finger across his phone's screen.

"Missy, you'll get along just fine without that old thing," her mom said. "You're getting to be a big enough girl."

"But Dolly's my only friend!" Missy felt a lump in her throat. It hurt and made it hard to swallow. Tears welled. "Can we please turn back?"

"I don't want to hear any more about that old thing." Her dad turned to look at her. "And no tears, am I clear?"

Missy nodded, and a tear spilled down each cheek.

"Some people go out of their way to show favoritism to every freak out there! The bigger the freak, the better. That's the way they like it." Gada's father sought them out in the rearview mirror again. "You kids ought to listen up back there."

Gada thought her father sounded angry. Was he mad at them? His words came out sounding higher, his tone tighter.

"No one's disagreeing with you," her mother said, trying to calm him. For this Gada felt thankful. She didn't like it when her father acted this way.

"I know, but trying to explain to those libtards that things are better this way is like trying to pull wisdom teeth with a plastic spoon. They drag their heels because they're scared of hurting anyone's feelings!"

Gada swept her crumpled-up food wrappers onto the floor, unbuckled her seat belt, and stretched out on the bench. The vehicle stank of fast food grease. The trip seemed to be taking forever.

She hoped seeing her wish granted would be exciting, but doubted it. She knew Missy would be there with her family, so she'd finally get her wish, but it also sounded like a bunch of people just sitting and listening to a bunch other people make speeches first.

"Not much longer, gang!" her father announced. "Only another two miles and we'll be there."

Gada closed her eyes. She twirled a ringlet of her hair with her index finger. It relaxed her. Gada's mother told her she used to do the same thing when she was a toddler.

"You're lucky," her mother once said back when life seemed more carefree. "You have such beautiful hair." Her mother had leaned down to plant a kiss on her daughter's forehead. Gada imagined she could feel that kiss now, so strong was the memory. Treatment would have made her lose her hair. Gada felt glad treatment had been banned. She closed her eyes and let her thoughts drift.

Sleep had just taken her when she awoke to her father saying, "Look at all these people, Gada! They're all here to see your wish come true."

"They'll destroy the country if we let them. The Leader is a blithering buffoon and his followers are idiots. We're regressing with each passing day."

Missy shifted in her seat. She needed to pee. She didn't want to say anything, though. Her dad would just tell her to hold it. Her mom murmured in agreement every time her father spoke, and Missy wondered if she really felt the same way or just pretended.

"And don't even get me started on all that gerrymandering and voter suppression," he said, and smacked the steering wheel with his hand.

Her eyes moved from her father to her mother, and then to Robert. They all had dark hair, matching brown eyes, and skin that tanned in the sun. She felt self-conscious, with her curly blonde hair, light blue eyes, and pale freckled skin. Gada had once asked her if she had been adopted. Missy's face had burned with embarrassment as she stammered her response. Gada had only sneered and turned away.

"The turnoff to the ceremony is half a mile ahead," her dad called. "Now remember: stick close together! I don't want anyone in the family getting separated. We'll hang back and see what this is all about."

Missy had to pee—bad. She took her seat belt off but that only made it worse. She felt like a water balloon filled too full.

"Dad, I have to use the bathroom," she moaned. "How much longer?"

"Didn't you hear me just now?" Her dad stared at her in the rearview mirror. "I just told you we're nearly there."

When they arrived, members of the security staff surrounded and ushered them to a special room behind the stage to wait for Gada's wish. When Missy saw the structure erected on the stage as they passed, she lost control of her bladder and erupted into sobs.

The Wish Granters Ceremony Script. These pages were found lying scattered in an adjacent alley following the event:

[PRE-SHOW MUSIC AND VENUE ANNOUNCEMENTS]

VENUE ANNOUNCER:

"Ladies and gentlemen, welcome your host for this morning's ceremony, Mason Crewell from Channel 2!"

[HOST ENTERS TO LECTERN]

MASON CREWEL:

"Good morning everyone, and welcome to the 5th Annual Wish Granters Ceremony! It is hard to believe we are celebrating this event's 5th anniversary already! Channel 2 has been involved since the beginning and we are a proud partner of Wish Granters. Today I am here, because, like you, I believe in the power and strength in granting a wish. I want to make sure that every eligible child facing a life-threatening medical condition here in the Black Mountains is able to have their wish granted. Each year, well over 600 wishes are granted.

"So, thank you for being here today and for believing in the Black Mountains Chapter of Wish Granters and its important mission of providing entertainment to sick kids and their families.

"We need to thank the people and organizations that helped make today's event possible. Please join me in thanking our leading sponsors: Esoteric Order Insurance, Flensman Exterminators, and Bathory Tools & Supply, as well as all the other sponsors you see listed on banners displayed throughout the town common!

"Let's give them a round of applause!"

[LEAD APPLAUSE, POINT OUT ANY NON-PARTICIPANTS TO SECURITY]

"Special thanks to our dedicated volunteer committee and volunteers who handled every detail to make this day perfect for the wish family. In addition, thanks to all of you for being here today! It makes me proud to see all of you lined up in front of me. I feel honored to be here.

"I also want to recognize Agnatha Tetsy, regional director of the Black Mountains Chapter of Wish Granters. Along with the volunteers, Agnatha coordinated today's event. Joining her today from the National Wish Granter Headquarters are Hector Damien, Volunteer and Outreach Director, and Paul Ghast, President and CEO."

[LEAD APPLAUSE, POINT OUT NON-PARTICIPANTS...]

"As you know, today's event is primarily a fundraiser. While we thank each of you who raised essential funds, we want to recognize a few of you who have exceeded every possible expectation. Leesa Caturia, representing our main sponsor, Esoteric Order Insurance, is here to help present awards. Thank you Leesa!"

LEESA:
"As we read your names, make your way to the front of the stage to be recognized. Please remain on stage until the last name gets called, then follow Mr. Ghast to the panel truck waiting next to the stage.

"As of 5:00 p.m. yesterday, we want to thank our number 5 fundraiser, _____ [APPLAUSE], our number four fundraiser, _____ [APPLAUSE], our number three fundraiser, _____ [APPLAUSE], our number two fundraiser, _____ [APPLAUSE], and the top individual fundraiser for the Black Mountains Chapter of Wish Granters, with more than $_____ raised, is _____!" [FINAL ROUND OF APPLAUSE, ESCORT ALL TO TRUCK]

"We also have some amazing teams out there, and I would like to recognize our top three fundraising teams. Number 3 is the _____. Number 2 is _____. And the top fundraising team for Wish Granters with more than $_____ raised, is _____!" [APPLAUSE, ESCORT TO TRUCK]

"Congratulations everyone! We know many of you have, or will, donate today and we want to thank you for your generous support. If you have not yet had the chance to give, gifts can be placed in the designated donation jars, at the merchandise tent, or at the donation table right here by the stage. Credit cards are also accepted at the merchandise tent. Help us reach our goal today of $85,000!"

[MUSICAL FANFARE—LEAD AND ENCOURAGE APPLAUSE.]

MASON:
"You will find Wish Kids in nearly every community. Unfortunately, kids everywhere face medical challenges that are sometimes heartbreaking, but unavoidable. We can draw

inspiration from their situations. And, as we will witness today, granting a wish has the side benefit of providing the rest of us with some wonderful entertainment!

"What all these sick and dying kids share is the unique experience of being a part of the Wish Granters family—one of the fastest growing organizations on the planet. Since the Black Mountains Chapter of Wish Granters started in 2024, more than 2,657 wishes have been granted. That is more than 2,657 Wish Kids and thousands upon thousands of family members who have been impacted by the work of Wish Granters.

"During the march, you will have a stop along the way at Gaston's Theatre to watch the powerful story of Thaddeus's wish, which was granted last summer. In addition, following the march today, you will have the chance to be part of a wish and see the magic for yourself. So be sure to come back following the march!

"At this time, we would invite ANY WISH KIDS here today to make their way to the front of the stage. If your Wish Kid is unable to be here or is no longer alive, we invite a Wish Parent or Wish Sibling to come up to represent the strength and bravery of your child. We will recognize all of you soon!"

[LEAD APPLAUSE]

"Today we celebrate wishes because EVERY child between the ages of 3 and 17 with a life-threatening medical condition deserves a granted wish.

"One of my favorite parts of Wish Granters is meeting our Wish Kids and their families. These are our real-life celebrities among us! A number are here today near the stage. Let's give them a big round of applause."

[LEAD APPLAUSE]

"Be sure to say 'hi' to the Wish Kids and ask them about their wishes. There are so many fun stories!

"As you march today, think about the kids and families standing here now, the 2,657 kids and families across the state who have had wishes granted, and all the kids waiting to have their wishes granted. There is so much more entertainment coming, believe me.

"Join us immediately after the march, as a special wish will be granted here today! Trust me; you don't want to want to miss this! There will also be music, food and drinks, with all proceeds going back the Black Mountains Chapter of Wish Granters. Also, take a moment to visit all our sponsor booths. Each one has a creative activity. And if you haven't had a chance to give yet and would like to, be sure to do so at the donation table near the stage, the merchandise tent, or in one of the designated donation jars.

"Now, as I mentioned earlier, we have a special stop today during the march. We will march from here and gather inside Gaston's Theatre to hear the story of Wish Kid Thad and his granted wish. Then we will proceed on our normal march route west down Saint Vitus Street. Just a reminder that when we get to Gaston's, it is important that you fill the front rows first and promptly take your seat.

"It's time to get started, so let's bring up Silas, one of our Wish Kids who is still with us, to help us count down. Silas faces an autoimmune disease, and he had his wish granted two summers ago. Boy, that TNT sure was fun, wasn't it, Silas?"

[PAUSE FOR CHEERS]

SILAS:
"5, 4, 3, 2, 1! Start marching!"

[MARCH TAKES PLACE]

[POST-MARCH]

MASON:
"Welcome back. I hope you enjoyed the march. Wasn't Thad's story powerful? And what a creative wish! Notice how organized Thaddeus stayed during his illness, and how he kept such thorough records of everyone he infected. It was also powerful to see the impact that Thad's revelation had on everyone involved. Thank you again to everyone who made his wish a reality.

"Now, before you enjoy the activities and the food, you are in for a treat. At this time, we would like to ask Wish Kid Gada Sneve and her parents Mat and La-Norr to come to the stage. Gada is six years old and lives near Stonewall. Gada's name means "lucky," and even though she has been diagnosed with terminal cancer, she's still lucky because today we will grant her wish!"

[LEAD APPLAUSE]

"We would also invite Wish Granter volunteers Marth and Sarai Odden, Johan Krispin from Scorch Steelworks, Bret Sammoth from Shackleford Blacksmiths, and Thomas Tribb from the Black

Mountains Fire Department to join us on stage. Here is Hector Damien from Wish Granters for the introduction…"

HECTOR:
"Thank you again for being here today. It is inspiring to see so many people from the area coming out to support our Wish Kids and their families. Our guest of honor is Gada Sneve. She's here today with her parents, and her big brother, Colby. Mat and La-Norr, could you tell us about Gada and her medical history?"

[MAT AND LA-NORR ANSWER]

HECTOR:
"What was your reaction when you found out the board chose her to receive a granted wish from Wish Granters?"

[MAT AND LA-NORR ANSWER]

HECTOR:
"What wish did Gada come up with and why?"

[AS MAT AND LA-NORR ANSWER, POINT OUT ANYONE WHO TRIES TO LEAVE.]

MASON:
"Again, we extend our thanks to each of our sponsors for your time and generosity in helping to make Gada's wish to come true! Now ladies and gentlemen, cheer as loud as you can as we bring out the subjects of Gada's wish: Missy Steuben, who is Gada's *least*-favorite classmate, and Missy's parents, Sam and Allie and her older brother, Robert!"

[LEAD APPLAUSE AS STEUBEN FAMILY IS LED TO AND SHACKLED INSIDE THE CAGE]

MASON:
"All right, it's time to make your wish come true, Gada. Soak 'em and light 'em!"

[NOTE: KEEP BACK TO AVOID BURNS]

[LEAD APPLAUSE AFTER]

[FINAL REMARKS]

MASON:
"Wow, what a morning! Again, enjoy the activities in the Square at all the sponsor booths, food and beverages, with all proceeds supporting Wish Granters. Also, stop by the merchandise tent to buy a t-shirt or souvenir photo of today's granted wish, or to make a donation if you have not already. Thank you to our sponsors and to all of you for being here today and for supporting the kids and families of the Black Mountains Chapter of Wish Granters!

"Let's have some more fun!"

[DIRECT GADA AND HER FAMILY TO THE CAGE FOR PHOTOS WITH THE CHARRED REMAINS. WHEN THIS IS COMPLETED, ESCORT YOURSELF TO THE PANEL TRUCK WAITING BEHIND THE STAGE.]

PEDESTRIAN ENCOUNTER

JUSTINE PLACED A CLEAN coffee mug on the drying rack. Her fingers, beginning to prune, searched the soapy dishwater and grasped a greasy skillet. She scrubbed in silence, her mind working out how best to defend against the World's Loudest Noise, which was scheduled for that evening.

When Justine looked out the window above the sink, she noticed the man. He stood on the sidewalk outside her gate, turned away from her, staring at the sky above the tree line.

In the living room, Justine's mother Ruth announced in a croaking singsong: "A house is made with walls and beams. A home is made with love and dreams."

"Sure, Mom," Justine murmured. She never knew when the old woman would dispense one of her timeworn maxims, simple wisdom gleaned from her childhood, perhaps the last things she remembered clearly.

Justine dried her hands on a dishtowel, her eyes never leaving the motionless figure.

"I need to run outside, Mom," Justine said. "There's a man on the sidewalk that looks like he needs directions." Then, though her mother wouldn't understand, she added, mostly to herself, "Or maybe he's worried about tonight."

Ruth did not reply. Justine left the house through the kitchen's battered screen door and followed the cement walk along the side of their home. She paused at the northeast corner of the house and observed the man. He remained on the sidewalk as if rooted to the spot.

Justine scrutinized the stranger. His salt and pepper hair was cut short and he wore slacks and a faded red polo. She couldn't see his face, and for a giddy moment pictured him without one, a flat, featureless cipher.

An urgent need to put this irrational fear to rest pressed her into motion. She strode across her small but well-maintained lawn.

"Can I help you?"

The man started at the sound of her speech and swiveled his head to watch her approach.

Justine noticed his eyes first, pastel blue and sorrowful. His receding hairline, drooping jowls, and the crow's feet framing his eyes betrayed his age, which Justine estimated as being about a decade younger than that of her mother.

"I don't see how you could."

"Well, I happened to notice you standing here..." Justine trailed off. A lone tear had spilled down his weathered left cheek. "You look familiar. Do I know you?"

The man roused himself. "Maybe. I live a few blocks down the street." He straightened and wiped away the tear with the back of a liver-spotted hand. "I'm sorry."

"You don't have to be sorry." Justine felt bad for staring. "It's all right to cry. It's healthy."

The man shook his head. "I'm sorry I'm here, sorry to inconvenience you." Another tear fell and this time he did not bother to brush it aside. "I think this whole damn country's going crazy."

"What's wrong?" Justine asked, though she thought she already knew.

The man gave her a look. "This thing scheduled tonight over at Getz Air Force Base. It's madness."

Justine glanced up and down the sidewalk. "I think so, too."

The man met her gaze with rheumy eyes. Justine felt her throat tighten as she spoke in hurried, hushed tones. "My mother's an invalid. We can't travel. But you and your family could still book a flight. Get as far away as you can before it happens."

"My wife and I already had that argument." He winced as if reliving the scene. "It became rather heated. She loves the idea of the World's Loudest Sound. She says she can't wait for it."

"I'm sorry to hear you and your wife are at odds," Justine said. "But I need to go back inside the house. My mother's mind wanders, and I should go check on her."

"Oh." The man's shoulders sagged. "Okay."

Justine had already made it halfway up the walk. She reentered the house and looked in on her mother. Ruth rocked in silence, her features serene. Justine returned to the sink. The soap bubbles had popped during her absence, leaving the remaining dirty dishes submerged in gray water. Reluctantly, she looked back out the window.

The man was leaning against her fence, like a drunken guard outside Buckingham Palace. Justine shut her eyes and wished the stranger away.

It didn't work.

"Why would I stick my neck out for someone I don't even know?" she muttered. "I need to be preparing for tonight." She would finish the dishes, and then begin experimenting with her canning wax. She wanted to fashion heavy-duty earplugs before tonight's event.

"Do unto others as you would have them do unto you."

Like countless times before, her mother had set her straight by quoting scripture. *Or was this the Golden Rule?* Justine sighed. "You're right, Mom, you're right."

With the Noise weighing heavy on her mind, Justine returned to the yard. The man turned when he heard her approaching.

"Would you like to come in for coffee?"

"Could I get a glass of water? I'm so mad my mouth has dried up." He paused and then said, "I'm Darren."

"Water for Darren, coffee for me, then."

"That sounds great." A wistful look spread across Darren's face like the shadows of clouds overhead. "Will your mother mind?"

"Not at all. She's kind of in her own little world."

Justine made two cups of instant coffee and rooted around in the kitchen cupboards until she found a half-empty box of crackers and a sleeve of Girl Scout cookies. She drew a glass of water from the tap for her visitor and dropped in a trio of ice cubes to cool his drink. She also added an ice cube to her mother's coffee so she wouldn't burn her tongue.

Darren received his glass of water with thanks and ate one of the cookies, though Justine thought he only did the latter to be polite. Ruth gummed her crackers and chuckled, caught up in the excitement of entertaining a guest.

"I wish they wouldn't do it," Darren said at last. He seemed to have calmed, resignation replacing his exasperation. "But if they insist, why not do it over the ocean somewhere? Why here?"

"Who knows? Maybe just because they can," Justine said. "Maybe to distract us from something else. Maybe to help sell earplugs."

"Well, good Lord!" Darren complained. "It's a colossal show, but for what purpose?"

Justine set her coffee mug aside and brushed a few crumbs from her mother's mouth. "It's 'sound and fury, signifying nothing'."

Darren smiled, "You said it, sister."

"Well, Shakespeare did, anyway." Justine remarked.

"I don't think Shakespeare's your sister," Ruth said, frowning as she studied their guest.

Justine, despite herself, laughed. She took her mother's hand and gave it a gentle squeeze. "This is Darren, Mom. He lives down the street."

"Of course he does," Ruth said. Then, turning to their guest, she added, "It's always nice to have you visit, dear."

Darren gave Ruth a lopsided smile.

"The World's Loudest Noise—who came up with that anyway?" Justine said, steering their conversation back to the topic at hand. "As if the idea itself isn't appalling enough, it sounds like a fourth grader came up with the name."

Darren nodded. "And not a particularly bright fourth grader, either."

"There's no underestimating the intelligence of the American people," Ruth said.

Both Justine and Darren stared at her. She brushed the last of her crumbs into a napkin with a gnarled hand and then leaned back and sat primly in her chair.

"This is doing her good," Justine said, looking at Darren. "Maybe you should visit more often."

"Maybe I will," Darren said. His features showed a new measure of resolve. "We just need to get through tonight."

Justine nodded. "I have a plan. I'm going to try and see if I can fashion heavy duty earplugs out of melted canning wax."

"Good luck. I hope it works." Darren rose. "Thank you both for your company." He bowed before Ruth, who only smiled uncertainly in response.

Justine saw him to the door, and then, on impulse, walked with him to her gate. Darren turned to face her. "Thank you."

An unexpected lump filled her throat. Justine tried to reply, but couldn't. Darren's face wavered, distorted by her brimming tears. She leaned in and hugged him fiercely, then stepped back inside her gate.

Darren shuffled away down the sidewalk.

Justine returned to her living room and cleared the dishes from the coffee table. The water in the sink had gone ice cold. She drew a shuddery breath and gazed out at the empty street.

Darren was right; it seemed like everyone *had* gone crazy. She felt like Alice, exposed to the grimmer, more dangerous side of Wonderland.

Justine felt grateful for her mother's presence. Ruth had always been there for her only daughter, imparting wisdom and giving advice the best way she knew how—in the form of recycled axioms and proverbs. Even as she succumbed to the disease that eroded a tiny piece of her mind with each passing day, the old woman always seemed to know exactly what her daughter needed to hear.

Justine returned to the living room, knelt at the base of the rocking chair and took one of Ruth's hands in each of her own. "This too shall pass," Ruth announced from her chair.

Like she'd done so often as a girl, Justine sat at the foot of her mother's rocker, watching television as the minutes ticked away. She massaged her temples and tried to make sense of it all: the president's announcement, the rabidly enthusiastic response of his supporters, and the military compliance. She'd listened to the talking heads bickering on television, where scathing sarcasm and vague threats offset effusive praise and anticipation. Justine ran through scenarios in her mind, imagining what she'd say if she unexpectedly had the entire country as her attentive audience.

The light in room, she realized, had dimmed.

Justine cast a sudden look at the clock above the mantle, and saw she had less than two minutes until the appointed time. She shot to her feet and ran to the kitchen in full panic mode.

There wasn't enough time to melt the wax. Justine clenched her hands into fists. Her nails bit into her flesh. Would foam earplugs be enough? She doubted it. Justine tried to remember her intentions regarding the protection of her eardrums, but all rational thought fled. She yanked open the junk drawer. It flew out all the way, scattering its contents across the floor in a colorful, clattering avalanche. Justine let the emptied drawer drop from numb fingers.

"Mother! Mom! What should I do?"

Before the old woman could respond, a sound rose in the growing dusk. Justine ground her teeth in frustration. She covered her ears with her hands, knowing it would do no good. She'd failed in her vigilance. The only thing she could do now was hope.

She curled into a fetal position on the kitchen linoleum as the Noise rose in volume. Each time Justine thought the roar couldn't get any louder, it did. It became unbearable, until one eardrum and then the other popped in quick succession. Even then, Justine felt in her body the sound's concussive, unrelenting force.

Please, Justine prayed. *Just let me hear her voice again.* She rose and steadied herself against the counter. Her cheeks were awash with tears. She sniffled and wiped her nose with the back of her hand. It came away smeared with wet crimson. She rapped her knuckles on the counter, but heard nothing, not even the ringing that comes with complete silence. She knew if she looked in the mirror, she'd see twin trickles of blood coming from each ear.

Shattered glass from the kitchen window had tumbled into the still-filled sink. An ambulance careened past. Justine saw its light rack flashing but heard no siren.

Her entire body shaking with apprehension, Justine picked her way across the refuse-strewn living room floor until she reached her mother's rocking chair.

Here, too, the tone had shattered windows. Ruth slumped to one side of her rocker. She held one hand over her heart, as if she meant to recite the pledge of allegiance, but her features were slack, her eyes glassy and vacant.

"Mom?" Perhaps she said the words, or perhaps she only thought them. *"Can you hear me? Are you there?"*

She watched her mother's face for signs of movement. She held trembling fingers to her mother's neck, feeling for a heartbeat. She felt none.

Then she heard it, her mother's voice, coming from somewhere behind the old woman, but not from her lips.

"No mother and daughter ever live apart, no matter what the distance between them."

Justine, cradling Ruth's motionless, already-cooling hands, sank to her knees and began to weep sweet tears of relief.

FEAR INCARNATE

LIGHTNING WASHED THE CABIN'S wood-paneled walls in eerie blue-white light.

"Damn that was bright!" Jennifer cried. She slowed her descent and Andy felt her fingertips press against his chest. "It lit up the entire—"

Then everything seemed to happen at once. The lamp, a victim of the strike, died and darkness reigned. A massive clap of thunder sounded, shaking the room. Jennifer rolled off him with frantic abruptness. Andy heard her land on the cabin's wood floor with a fleshy thump. "Oh my god!"

Andy sat up in bed. He squinted but couldn't see her. "It's all right, it's just a thunderstorm."

"No, it's *not* all right." Jennifer spoke from somewhere in the darkness below and side him, sounding as if she was trying to hold back sobs. She had moved away from the bed and Andy could now make out her vague shape cowering near the wall, opposite the window. He peered around the room, trying to understand the situation.

"I have candles," he said, still feeling lost. "No need to panic."

Jennifer seemed not to hear. "We're in trouble."

"I'm sure everything's fine." *Where are my damn glasses?*

"I saw my husband out there!" This time a sob did follow Jennifer's words. "He must have followed me." She reached for her blouse.

Andy's mouth went dry. *That drunken gun nut, Darrell? She saw him? Shit.*

"Looking in the window at us?" His tongue felt thick in his mouth but he forced out the words. "Are you sure?"

"Yes!" She crawled toward the bedroom door, staying low.

Andy squinted at the window. He fumbled a hand across the nightstand, searching for his glasses. *Did they fall on the floor?*

Jennifer had finished dressing in record time and had left the room. Andy peered again at the window. The vague shapes of tree branches waved amid flashes of lightning. Andy shivered and swung his legs out of bed.

More lightning flashes filled the room with a paparazzi-like fervor. Jennifer's bare feet slapped on the wood floor in the outer room. Her pacing, like an imprisoned wild animal, sent a fresh set of chills through him. Without warning, Jennifer's footfalls broke into a run. The sounds of the storm increased, and the atmosphere of the bedroom became damp and cool. But that wasn't possible unless—

"Did she just *leave?*" Andy asked the empty room.

He stood beside his bed, eyes wide, mouth open. A gust wind caught the open door and slammed it against the cabin wall like a gun shot.

Andy bolted toward the door.

Panic had driven her from the safety of the cabin, and it was too late to turn back. Pine needles stabbed at the soles of her feet and icy droplets of rain pelted her skin. Jennifer raced through the darkness toward the foot of the driveway where she had left her car. With each lightning flash, she expected Darrell to emerge from behind a tree. What would she do then? *Gotta get to my car. Grab the .22 he bought me. And if I can't load the damn thing in time, I'll just run him over.*

A flash of lightning illuminated the night and a dark form loomed in Jennifer's path. A yelp escaped her lips as she tried to change direction. Her feet slipped on the rain-slicked carpet of pine needles and she slammed into the ground, the air knocked from her lungs.

She lay on the wet earth, fighting for oxygen, feeling the way she imagined carp felt when anglers tossed them on riverbanks to die. Jennifer opened her eyes. *Might as well look the drunken jackass in the eye when he kills me.*

But the looming figure, now off to her right, had not moved.

Just a dead tree. She thought it might have been the burned-out trunk of a birch tree that had been struck by lightning during some previous storm but felt no inclination to look closer.

Darrell was still out there, she reminded herself. She'd seen him glaring in the window at her—at *them.* He'd seen her astride the owner of the cabin. Andy was a mutual acquaintance; sweet and caring, but soft. Jennifer didn't think he was man enough to fight off a direct attack from her husband. And if Darrell had brought along any of his guns, none of them stood much chance of survival.

There! She brushed wet strands of her dark hair away from her eyes. Her sedan, which she'd backed into the driveway after seeing the turn a split-second too late, sat at the end of the drive. Jennifer judged the distance at less than thirty yards. She clambered to her feet, and staggered toward the vehicle, brushing mud, leaves and needles from her skin as she moved.

Gun's in the glove box...

Instead of reassuring her, the words increased her panic. She broke into a run. Was that her heart or the pounding of approaching footsteps? Overhead, trees loomed. Thunder boomed. She pumped her arms and churned her legs.

Almost there! The distance between her and the potential safety of her car dwindled. Envisioning herself slipping again and sliding headfirst into the side of the automobile, she slowed. Jennifer kept her footing and cast a frantic glance over her shoulder before pulling the passenger door handle.

Nothing happened.

She yanked the handle again. *Locked. Damn it!* She tried the rear passenger door with the same maddening result.

Jennifer resisted the urge to scream. If she lost her head, she might as well sign her own death certificate. She had to think this through.

The keys are in my purse back up at the cabin. Even though the passenger doors are all locked, the driver's side might be unlocked.

She couldn't drive away, but she could still get the gun out of the glove box. She hurried around the hood of her car and reached for the door's handle. At that moment another thought occurred to her.

I should have looked under the car first.

I can't see a damned thing.

Fate had dealt him no lights, missing glasses, and a night spiraling out of his control. Andy raced from the bedroom, through the kitchen, and slammed the front door on the rain. For a moment, he stood there torn. Should he follow Jennifer, try to lead her back to safety? Or lock the door on any potential lurking danger? He swallowed and felt surprised at the dry click in his throat. He reached out and twisted the deadbolt.

Andy hurried back to the bedroom. He skipped his socks and pulled on his sneakers. He stood and something cracked under his foot. He knelt and he scooped up his misplaced glasses. *Broken. That figures.*

Andy crept to the window. The rain continued, but he saw fewer flashes of lightning, heard less thunder. He wondered how long before the electric company restored power. He peered into the darkness but didn't feel confident about seeing anything—unless it leapt into view right in front of his face. This thought painted a mental picture he didn't care for at all, so he pushed the image away.

He didn't own a gun. For protection, a steak knife from the silverware drawer was the best he'd be able to do.

No one lurked beneath her car, but Jennifer's relief proved short-lived.

A prolonged roar from the surrounding woods raised the hair on the nape of her neck and sent goose pimples rippling over her flesh.

Darrell, you sound like you've gone out of your mind!

She wondered if Andy was hurt—or even dead—at the hands of her husband. She had wasted seven unhappy years with that man. Darrell's excessive drinking, coupled with his violent temper, made her day-to-day existence miserable. His vices created and shaped her vices. He didn't understand emotional fulfillment, or her need to feel desirable. He understood only rage. He wanted to control her every move, but never tried to control his own anger. Now he'd discovered her infidelity. He would make her pay for her transgressions—of this, she felt sure.

Jennifer vowed to put a stop to his abuse. Tonight, she would defend herself. She could certainly justify shooting him now; he sounded like a crazed animal.

She thought again of the way he had glared in at her through the cabin window. Gaunt, hollow-eyed and mean, with his upper lip curled in the sneer she hated and feared. The sneer that meant he would soon punish her with his fists, or his belt, or a burning cigarette...

She reached out, yanked the door handle, and the car door sprang open. Holding her elation in check, Jennifer slid behind the wheel and pulled the door closed. She slammed the door lock down, leaned across the seat, and opened the glove box. Perched atop a collection of receipts, expired proof-of-insurance cards, and vehicle registration slips, sat the handgun Darrell had bought for her two years prior. *A Springfield something-or-other. He'd be pissed if he knew I forgot.*

Gasping with relief, Jennifer removed the weapon from its holster. Then she reached into the glove box again, pawing through papers until her fingers touched the ammunition clip. It had slipped behind the stack of detritus and fallen to the bottom of the glove box.

Jennifer slammed the clip home, chambered a round, and looked at the car's windows in sudden dismay. The glass had fogged. *He could walk right up to the car and I wouldn't see him!*

She toggled the safety to the off position and threw open her car door. The rain had stopped, but clouds still obscured the moon and stars. Tall conifers towered in the darkness around her like silent members of some occult council. Jennifer glanced back at the condensation-obscured windows and inspiration seized her.

I'll do what no one would expect me to do. She dropped to the ground, careful to keep her weapon elevated and dry, and slid between the rain-soaked gravel and the undercarriage of her car. She ignored the scraping discomfort of the muddy gravel and wriggled until she felt concealed. She could watch the path that wound up the hill toward Andy's cabin. When Darrell came toward her, she'd be ready.

I'm going to bushwhack your sorry ass, hon.

She didn't wait long.

A figure emerged from the forest. Her husband, his cruel eyes blazing, strode straight toward her hiding spot. Dark hilarity twisted his features, and even in darkness evil intentions radiated from his form like heat waves on a desert highway.

Her tormentor, elongated and shadow-like, towered over her, impossibly tall. With each step, he grew in size, twisting into an inhuman, hulking nightmare.

Rational thought retreated, allowing animal instinct to take center stage. The postganglionic neurons of her central nervous system flooded her tissue with norepinephrine. Her eardrums thrummed as if she sat atop a wailing tornado siren.

That's not Darrell at all. That's something else, something... other. Her beating heart seemed to pummel itself against her ribcage. *That... that....*

Her arm followed the directive of her fight-or-flight response. She aimed the handgun and pulled the trigger.

Once proved enough.

Andy heard the shot. Against his better judgment, he walked to the door and pulled it open. He inched his way out of the cabin.

The winds had slackened. Clouds still scudded across the cool night sky, but the rain had stopped. Droplets still trickled from the branches of the trees and the roof of the cabin. Andy reached the gravel driveway and stopped short. Darkness and his astigmatism blurred most of the detail, but he thought he saw someone standing at the foot of the driveway next to Jennifer's car. Andy pressed his lips together and tried to maintain control over his breathing. He slid into the shadow beside the cabin.

That could be Jennifer down there, but he didn't think so. More likely it was her vengeful husband. Andy didn't want to invite any more trouble than he already had. And if the sound he'd heard *had* been a gunshot...

Andy stood, irresolute. The figure had disappeared. His ears strained for some indication of what was happening down at the foot of the drive. At last, he could stand it no longer. He needed to act, to formulate a plan.

A pang of regret came with the realization that he didn't have his own transportation. He'd let Jennifer drive them to their secluded rendezvous, at the time thinking that if he supplied the location, she could spend the gas to get them there.

Playing a hunch, he went back into the cabin and rummaged through Jennifer's forgotten purse. He grinned as his hand seized on a key fob. He knew the lay of the land and felt confident in his ability to approach Jennifer's vehicle undetected. He'd creep up, sneak a peek, and then decide what to do. If she was there waiting for him, they'd jump in her car and drive to town, straight to the police station. If she wasn't there? *Same plan.*

Andy exited his cabin and crept from tree to tree, pleased with the soggy pine needles' cooperation in keeping his passage silent. He circled the trunk of a dead birch and pondered the night's events. Drama like this didn't happen to people like him. Normal guys who—

Andy stopped short. Jennifer's vehicle nestled in darkness compounded by shadow about twenty-five yards down the incline of the hill. Silence reigned. He had no delusions about seeing anything in detail. Instead, he crouched and gazed at the tableau before him, waiting and watching for one specific characteristic: movement.

He counted to one hundred, saw no activity, and counted to one hundred a second time. At last, he rose and made his way with caution and care toward Jennifer's car. It was a four-door sedan, nondescript and practical.

There's a something under the car, behind the front tire.

Damn it.

This thought was the closest Andy had come to a prayer in at least a decade. Now he found himself wishing for divine intervention, hoping for a favor he knew he didn't deserve. He dreaded looking, but knelt and tilted his head sideways. He had to check, had to make sure she wasn't just playing possum.

"Jennifer, it's me. Andy."

She lay face down in the muck. This close, he could see strands of hair clinging to the car's undercarriage in a cobweb of gore.

Jesus Christ! She shot herself? Why?

His gorge rose and he clambered away from the body. His limbs felt weak and shaky. He stifled shocked sobs until his throat ached. He didn't dare weep. Remaining silent became his top priority. If he was lucky, maybe her husband was up in the cabin by now. But if he was lurking just within the tree line, watching...

Half a minute had passed when Andy realized he wasn't alone. He hadn't yet caught a glimpse, hadn't heard any telltale sounds, and yet something in the air had changed. If he turned, he'd see whatever had lurked at his cabin window.

Andy realized, with preternatural assurance, that Jennifer's husband had not followed them. Whatever had intruded upon their tryst was not some*one*, but some*thing*. He felt caught in a nightmare-spell of mounting terror that could only be broken by facing whatever insidious menace pursued him. The prospect terrified him.

Andy lunged for the car door, threw it open, and slid behind the wheel. His shaking hand fumbled in his jeans pocket. He dared not look up. Instead, he pulled out Jennifer's car key and jammed it into the ignition. He twisted it and the sedan's engine surged to life.

Andy threw the car into reverse and stomped on the gas pedal. The tires spumed up clots of mud as the vehicle lurched and then shot backwards toward the main road. Andy slammed on the brakes. He recognized Jennifer's pale, oblong shape lying in the muck. Something else stood in the middle of the path that led back up to his cabin. Andy sensed more than saw the creature's malevolence, felt it reaching out for him, trying, he realized, to scare him.

It took a shambling step forward.

Don't look at it.

All he had to do was back up onto the main road and drive away. He wouldn't get far without headlights though. Andy scanned the dashboard.

You don't *want to see it, though. If you look at it, it's got you trapped.*

He found the knob he sought and turned it, illuminating the road—and the approaching figure. It now stood much closer, and Andy found himself looking at it despite his fervent desire not to. The form wavered, defying logic by seeming to change shape, as if trying on and rejecting different forms. Andy clutched the wheel. The mounting terror held him paralyzed. The figure, nebulous yet appalling, had reached the hood of the car.

Eyeballs, a dozen or more on long sinewy stalks, tilted closer to the windshield. A six-sided maw opened, and an obscene, maggot-laden tongue unfurled and landed on the hood with a fleshy thump.

Andy's heart hurt, in a literal sense. The pain stabbed at him, drew him back to reality. He gasped for breath and killed the headlights. The loss of his night vision, combined with his poor eyesight, obscured just enough detail to break the creature's spell.

He pressed the accelerator with his foot and the car rolled

backwards until its rear tires found the smoother surface of the paved road. Andy moved his foot to the brake pedal. The figure, he noted, stood motionless, seemingly content to let him escape.

A vivid image arose in his mind's eye: a memory of the two of them together in his bed, sharing a moment of happiness they'd never have again. Relief gave way to rage. He put the sedan in neutral and pressed the gas pedal to the floor. The engine roared. He bellowed along with it. The figure ahead of him did not move. Andy wanted it to feel afraid, but it projected no outward indication of fear.

He shifted out of neutral and into drive. Wet gravel shot into the air as the sedan catapulted forward, gaining speed, hurtling straight toward the fear-mongering figure.

"I've got you now, you son of a bitch."

The fender struck the creature's legs—*too hard!* His subconscious warned—and it splayed across the hood, hitting the windshield with enough force to shatter the glass.

The sedan skidded to a stop. Andy found himself face to face, and eye to long-stalked eye, with fear incarnate.

With his final breath, he did the only thing he could.

Scream.

THE SODBUSTER AND THE SPIDER

"Long ago, a Lakota Sioux spiritual leader was on a high mountain and he had a vision. In his vision, Iktomi—the great trickster—appeared in the form of a spider. As Iktomi spoke, he took the elder's willow hoop and began to spin a web."—Lakota legend

WADE NORMAN'S FATHER DROWNED on dry land. It happened in the springtime. When Walter Norman did not appear for supper, Wade's mother, Edith, sent the boy out to look for him. Wade found his father lying on his back in the barn's hayloft, an empty rye bottle lying beside him in the golden straw. The older man appeared to have finished off the bottle and fallen asleep. He'd vomited, his body rejecting the bitter liquid, but enough trickled down his trachea that he suffocated and died. Sturgeon's doctor, Douglas Stuart, had coined the phrase that clung like a burr to Wade's thoughts.

"I'm sorry, my boy, but your pa found a way to drown on dry land."

Five months had passed since that bleak day. Wade had hoeing and planting to keep him busy the rest of the spring and plowing followed in the fall. The livestock needed tending every morning and evening. Wade worked from dawn to dusk if the weather was bad and longer when the weather was good.

On the September day that he rode his pony to Sturgeon for supplies, his mother lay abed inside their homestead cabin, coughing her life away, a few burgundy droplets at a time.

Wade's lank brown hair tumbled down his forehead just enough to provide his squinting blue eyes a measure of shade from the fiery orb soaring imperceptibly across the sky. He did not own a hat, but wished he did.

His sunburned, windblown features would have looked appropriate on a thirty-year-old man, but not on a twelve-year-old boy. His chest was white as cow's milk, but his forearms had browned beneath the sun. His face was too gaunt to be considered handsome—only his eyes retained any spark of the lingering innocence and exuberance of youth.

Wade reached town intent on his task. He was supposed to obtain medicine, something to help his mother rest, from Doctor Stuart. His mother had also given him a short list of items to obtain from the grocer. Wade's pony plodded to a hitching post and the boy dismounted and wrapped the reins around the horse-chewed wood.

Townsfolk strolled along the boardwalks. Two dogs fought over a chicken carcass stripped of its meat. From unseen trees, cicadas sang their shrill song.

Then something remarkable happened.

An imposing-looking man rode into view. He sat on his saddle, Wade thought, like a king on his throne. He rode down the middle of the dusty street with chin up and chest out. The stranger pulled the reins, and his stallion—the color of the ash and coals of a dead campfire—pranced a moment and then stood still.

The newcomer scanned the assembling crowd. One hand stroked a trimmed mustache and goatee then dropped and settled on the butt of a pearl-handled revolver holstered low on his thigh. A reverent hush fell upon the group of townsfolk that had quickly assembled like ants around a dropped dollop of strawberry jam. Wade stood among them. The stranger lifted his hand from the revolver and brushed travel dust from the silver star affixed to his duster's lapel. Everyone waited in silence until the lawman spoke.

"I am Marshal Eugene Masters," he boomed, "and I've come to your town to serve as God's wrath."

Gasps erupted from several of those assembled. Even the town sheriff, a squat fellow with a ruddy face named Holst, gaped in apparent astonishment. A few of Sturgeon's more notorious drunkards put away their flasks. Gummy Kate, a soiled dove, looked abashed and drew her ratty shawl over her mostly-exposed bosom. Even the cicadas fell into respectful silence.

Marshal Masters favored the assembled throng with a tight-lipped smile and continued. "God's law has been broken. Man's law has been broken. About ten miles south of here, as the buzzard flies, a family of homesteaders has been brutally massacred."

Shocked murmurs rippled through the crowd. Someone said, "God have mercy on their souls."

The lawman straightened in his saddle and cocked his head, as if listening for instruction from the heavens. A sliding cloudbank hid the sun and darkened the street. Masters picked up the thread of his narrative and yanked it forward with the words: "All massacred, except for one."

Masters waited for the excited murmurs of the townsfolk to subside before resuming.

"One young girl, Alice Chambers by name, was spared by the grace of God. She hid while the outrageous acts of violence were carried out upon her kin. I will discover the culprits and bring them to swift justice. This, I solemnly vow."

The crowd, like a congregation of evangelicals, had started responding with increasing zeal each time the marshal paused.

"I will bring the cold-blooded, bloodthirsty cowards to justice!"

The murmurs became angry shouts of approval.

"I will not rest until the murderers are dead themselves and serving an eternal sentence in hell!"

Marshal Masters paused and used a neckerchief to wipe sweat from his brow as the crowd shouted and clamored.

"People of Sturgeon: When the time comes, will you be prepared?"

Shouts of assent came, but the marshal wasn't done. "When I come to you with information about the murderers, will you be ready to volunteer? Will you take up arms and dispense justice?"

His chest heaved amid the swelling roar of the crowd. Some scattered, perhaps returning to their homes intent on retrieving their guns. Others pushed closer to the marshal, trying to touch him, to touch his horse, or get in a word.

Wade let the frenzied men and women jostle past him. He gazed up at the lawman with unabashed admiration.

He'd found a hero.

That night, after completing his chores and giving his mother a teaspoon of her medicine, Wade fell upon his straw-filled mattress and plummeted into an exhausted sleep.

Reverend Gentry stood before him, austere and rigid. Wade had spent many Sundays watching in terrified fascination as the scowling reverend read long passages from his battered Bible, rebuking his sweating congregation with Old Testament tales of God's wrath. Now, however, the little country church, lit by a single guttering candle, housed only two occupants.

Wade sat ramrod straight in the front pew. The reverend addressed him in a hectoring, feverish tone. "It comes like a silk doll on rickety corncobs. His face pales to reach the color gray— dust dancing with dead leaves. The void increases when you get excited."

The words made little sense to Wade. Aware at a subconscious level that he was dreaming, he relaxed and simply nodded whenever Gentry paused.

Reverend Gentry gestured for him to come forward and kneel at the communion rail. Wade obeyed. The man of scripture held out a morsel of sacramental bread and the boy opened his mouth to receive it. Gentry pressed it onto his tongue and Wade felt an immediate change. His tongue was melting. Not daring to spit out the Lord's flesh, Wade swallowed the sacrament—along with the dissolving remnants of his tongue.

He gazed up at Reverend Gentry with wide and pleading eyes. The old man leaned in close and spoke in the voice of Walter Norman.

"God has taken away your tongue so you remember to keep your ears open. Serve him well with this gift bestowed."

Wade looked around with a sense of shock. A cool stream and rocky shore had replaced the darkened church. Wade had a moment to register the russet, craggy expanse of canyon walls. Then a giddy feeling of vertigo threatened to overwhelm him as the ground flew away from his feet.

Wade knew what would happen next. The hallmark of all bad dreams was the rapid ascent, followed by the terrifying plunge into wakefulness.

Instead, he rose only a few feet and the motion stopped. Wade found himself standing and staring at the wrinkled face of a weeping elder from one of the area tribes. Cheyenne, perhaps, or

Lakota.

Wade meant to make a polite inquiry on the subject but snapped his mouth shut, his teeth clacking together like a steel animal trap. No tongue meant no talking. As Wade looked on, the wizened face dissolved and reassembled. Eyes blinked and revealed caves. The old man's skin became russet canyon walls, down which twin waterfalls fell. Black hair erupted into a murder of crows flapping past Wade, their wings battering the air. One crow shot straight toward him, its beak sprung open as if to pluck out one of his eyes.

Wade woke and sat upright, gasping. His heart rattled his rib cage like a panicked prisoner until his eyes adjusted to the darkness of the cabin. In the next room, his mother snored. Crickets chirped. Above him, shining in the moonlight, hung a magnificent orb-shaped spider's web.

Before sleep reclaimed him, the boy bit down on his tongue to make sure it was still there.

Marshal Eugene Masters, though no longer in town, was still on the lips and in the minds of many of the townsfolk. Most of the men admired and wished to emulate him. Several of Sturgeon's fairer sex daydreamed about his piercing eyes, broad chest, and commanding yet soulful demeanor. Silent, secret fantasies abounded.

For Wade's part, he longed for a chance to impress the marshal. Two mornings after his startling dream, a remarkable opportunity presented itself.

He'd ridden to town to seek Dr. Stuart's advice regarding his mother. The man of medicine, to his credit, went straight to the truth. "She has consumption, Wade," he said. "The medicine I prescribed isn't going to cure anything. It will ease her suffering and help her rest, nothing more."

The enormity of the revelation left Wade with a painful lump in his throat. He vowed not to cry in the doctor's presence. He would ride all the way home and ensconce himself in the privacy of the root cellar before he let his tears fall.

Dr. Stuart gave Wade a reassuring pat on the back. "Chin up, my boy. At least you're old enough to make it on your own." His voice dropped to a murmur. "Not like that poor girl whose family got killed."

At this, Wade looked up, interested despite his sorrow. "Alice Chambers?"

"Yes, she's staying with my wife and me until we are able to determine her next of kin. Never says a word, not that I blame her. Sheriff Holst tried to question her about what happened that night. Marshal Masters has, too. She won't talk. This is rather vexing, and not only from a health and well-being standpoint. What if something she saw or heard could help bring the killers to justice?" The older man regarded Wade over the top of his wire-rimmed spectacles. He took a deep breath, held it as if considering something, and then let the air escape his lungs. "Wade, Alice is eight years old. I know you're twelve, and I know you've had to do a lot of growing up lately, but do you think you might be willing...?"

Stuart let the question hang in the air unfinished because Wade had already nodded in assent. Perhaps he wanted Wade to play games with the girl in an attempt to lift her spirits. Or perhaps he wanted him to counsel Alice, to help her cope with her situation. Wade yearned to meet her. He hoped to be the one to get her to open up, to reveal something of importance. He flushed at the thought of gaining an audience with Marshal Masters and presenting newfound evidence. He'd be a hero. Wade wondered how old one had to be before they could be deputized.

Dr. Stuart drew him back to reality by rising. "You could follow me there now, if you're inclined. You could meet Alice."

Wade nodded and rose. Outside, he mounted his horse and followed Dr. Stuart's carriage, feeling both excited and nervous to meet the orphaned girl.

When they arrived, Alice Chambers cowered in a corner of the Stuarts' sitting room. She was so petite she looked to Wade like a doll someone had discarded. He felt a twinge of momentary surprise at the girl's dark skin. His limited life experience had led him to assume she'd look like him.

"Alice, this is Wade Norman." Dr. Stuart gestured toward him. The girl eyed him with obvious mistrust. Stuart's wife, a tree stump of a woman with eyes that glowed with kindness, came in from the kitchen, wiping her hands on a dishtowel. Sturgeon's doctor knelt before the girl. "Wade's lost his daddy too. He... he wanted to say hello and offer his condolences."

The girl's eyes moved from her temporary benefactor back to Wade. His cheeks flushed. Not knowing what else to do, he walked across the room and sat down on the floor beside the miserable girl.

"Deep down in my heart, it hurts all the time." Wade wasn't aware he meant to speak until the words had left his mouth. Stuart gave him a curious look and Wade's cheeks burned even more. Then he felt the girl slide her tiny hand into his. She squeezed. He squeezed back. In that moment, Wade knew they'd formed an unspoken bond.

Dr. Stuart stood and followed his wife from the room. Soon Wade smelled coffee brewing. He and Alice sat in companionable silence, drawing strength from each other. He glanced at her and saw the telltale glisten of tears on her cheeks. He knew if she looked at him, she would see the same. Eventually, their breathing fell into a synchronous rhythm.

Time passed. The sun's path altered the shadows in the room. Wade felt his legs grow numb from the floorboards but didn't move. He didn't want to leave Alice's side. Dr. Stuart looked in on them from time to time, but for the most part let them have their privacy. Wade never let go of her hand.

Then, at the sound of chairs scraping the floor in the kitchen, Alice shocked Wade by leaning sideways and whispering into his ear.

"When it happened, I think I fainted, because I don't remember anything. I woke up hearing *pik-pik, pik-pik.* Like the coal miners back east swinging pickaxes. And then the sounds just faded away."

She sank back into her previous position. Wade felt too stunned to move. He tried to formulate a response, but the concept of words seemed to have fled his brain. Dr. Stuart entered the room.

"I shouldn't have kept you so long, Wade. Your mother must be worried sick." He grimaced, perhaps at his choice of words. His eyes moved from one child to the other. "I think you'd best be heading home."

Wade mounted his horse and rode back through town in the direction of the homestead. Chores awaited, not to mention tending to his mother. She would need a meal prepared, water heated for bathing, her medicine administered. Wade urged his horse into a gallop.

Two hours later, Wade sat beside his ailing mother. After explaining the reason for his late arrival, he had brushed his horse and bedded it down for the night, fed the livestock, and collected eggs from the chicken coop. Once his duties outdoors were complete, he returned to his mother's side, feeling conflicted about being away from home for so long.

Edith reached for his hand and he took it. Her fingers were cold and seemed to be all knuckles. "I'm glad you sat with that girl. My heart just breaks for her. You're a fine son, Wade." His mother's voice sounded whispery and paper thin. "And you'll grow into a good, kind man. A mother knows."

Wade didn't know how to respond so he gave her hand a gentle squeeze and remained at her side until she fell asleep. Then he rose and set about putting the cabin to rights for the night. At last, exhaustion overtook him, and Wade extinguished the last candle, kicked off his boots and stretched out on his own bed. He lay with hands clasped behind his head. The spider's web above him came into focus. Wade contemplated its complex, yet comforting pattern until sleep claimed him.

Wade stood in the barnyard. The sinking red sun touched the horizon. Wind sent dust and sand hissing through the overgrown weeds. He craned his neck, took in the enormity of the barn. Time and inclement weather had colluded to beat the boards to a disconsolate gray. How had he allowed this to happen? Wade reached out and pulled the barn door open. Dank, stale air filled his lungs. The sound of beating wings fluttered from rafter to rafter.

In the deep darkness, something moved, and Wade felt his chest constrict with fear. Dread saturated his thoughts, deadened his limbs. The shape, a black-on-black shadow in the far corner of the barn, drew closer. Wade became aware of an unsteady shuffling. It grew louder as the shape emerged from the darkness, approaching him.

The hairs on the back of his neck stood on end. Animal fear escaped his lips in an inarticulate moan. He tried to run, but couldn't. A horse loomed, lurching forward on stiff legs. Hollow sockets of darkness hung where its eyes should have been. The horse's hide clung to its ribs. Hipbones and spine protruded. Clumps of mane had fallen out. Flies shadowed the beast in a loose cloud.

Wade recognized the coal-and-ashes hide of the marshal's stallion. The creature came to a stop a mere two feet from him. Wade could have reached up to stroke the stallion's emaciated muzzle if he felt like it.

He didn't.

The horse lacked eyes, yet seemed to gaze at Wade just the same. The boy could only stare back in awe. This horse had every appearance of having been locked in the barn to starve. Based on the state of the barn, it had stood derelict for decades. How could the horse still be clinging to life? And for what purpose had it miraculously staved off death?

Before Wade could formulate an answer to these questions, the horse turned away from him. As its flank came between him and the setting sun, the red light of the orb shone through the stallion's rib cage.

The animal, he now realized, was little more than a reanimated skeleton, with tattered remnants of hide clinging to its bones. An object fell from a rear hoof as the horse hobbled back into the barn, swallowed by darkness.

Wade stooped and reached out for the object that had tumbled into the dust. It was a rusted horseshoe. Before his trembling fingers made contact, the horseshoe vanished.

Wade woke up in his bed. The cold gray light of impending dawn seeped in through the window. Chores awaited him. Sighing, Wade kicked his blanket aside and reached for his boots.

After working outdoors all morning, Wade looked in on his mother. He found her sitting up in bed, claiming to feel better. Wade thought he noticed a bit of color in her cheeks and felt grateful for the improvement.

He busied himself with minor cleaning inside the cabin, talking with his mother as he worked. He tried to improve her mood by bringing up pleasant memories from his childhood. He swept and scrubbed the floors, shook out rugs, and gave Edith a spoonful of medicine when she started feeling unwell.

Later, as she dozed, Wade entered his own tiny room. Here he also cleaned, needing to keep busy. He searched the ceiling for the spider's web but found nothing. He craned his neck trying to catch the web in the light without success.

Frowning, he gave up, pulled on a wool coat, and went outside to get a head start on the evening chores.

When Wade crawled into bed that night, the spider's web came into focus. He thought about getting up again to dispose of it, but his limbs felt heavy from the day's labors and he decided to wait until morning. He closed his eyes for a time, and then reopened them.

A spider descended from the web, looming large as it neared his face. Wade wanted to roll out of the way but found he could not.

"You are wise," the spider said, "and yet still have much to learn."

The orb-shaped web had blurred as Wade focused on the spider itself. The creature's abdomen shimmered with brilliant silver-white, green, and gold.

"I shall tell you two truths and one lie," the spider said. "Or perhaps, two lies and one truth. But we should relocate first."

Wade blinked and then gasped. He now sat in the hayloft where his father had died. His legs dangled out over the edge of the open hatch. He began to scramble to safety when the voice came again.

"No need to move."

Wade froze. He wanted to talk, to ask questions, but no words would come. In front of his face, illuminated by the moonlight, the spider swayed on a translucent thread.

"Listen to my words. You already have knowledge within you that can help save lives," the spider said. "The marshal is a good man who will listen when you bring him your message. Your mother will make a full recovery. Alice Chambers will soon be reunited with relatives."

Wade felt distress mounting within him. He wanted to do the right thing, but feared losing his mother most of all. He tried to follow the strands of logic, but his mind reeled.

"Do you know how to wake from a dream, lad?" The spider asked.

Wade nodded. "Yes, please."

"You better do it quick." The eight-legged creature ascended into the darkness. Wade heard something rustling in the hay behind him. Rats? Boards creaked. No. Not rats. Dread kept him frozen a few moments more. Then he twisted his head and saw a silhouetted figure shambling toward him.

Please don't let that be my father.

But it was.

Terrified, Wade pushed off with his hands and plunged through the open hatch. Instead of breaking his neck on a hayrack, he awoke in his bed gasping and drenched with sweat.

Of the spider's web, he saw no sign.

Wade knew exactly what he intended to tell Marshal Masters, he just had to find him first. This thought chased him through his day, like the catchy refrain of a Stephen Foster song.

Edith had taken a turn for the worse, it seemed, and Wade doted on her. As evening approached, he rushed through his chores, prepared a meal his mother barely touched, and then saddled his pony and headed for town. The man in the moon smiled down on him, as if proudly urging him onward.

The search for Masters proved to be an easy one. The noisy saloon was the only building still lit when he arrived. Wade recognized the marshal's stallion tied to a hitching post.

He dismounted, wound his pony's reins to another post, and climbed the two wooden steps to the saloon's batwing doors. The unmistakable booming voice of Marshal Masters sounded, not from the saloon's interior, but from somewhere above Wade. The boy moved out from under the awning and looked up.

The marshal's voice came again, and peals of laughter followed. Masters was not in the saloon after all, it seemed. Wade checked the side of the building and found a set of wooden stairs leading up to the second level. He ascended the stairs, not daring to look down. Ever since he'd discovered his father dead in the hay loft, Wade didn't react well to elevated heights. He had important information to pass along to the marshal, however, and refused to turn back.

Inside the room atop the saloon, the marshal sat with a tumbler in one hand and a lit cigar in the other. Several women who Wade guessed were dance hall girls lounged around him. An assortment of other hangers-on filled the cramped quarters. Among them, Wade noticed a few hard-eyed men who looked like gunslingers. Cobwebs hung from the rafters and tobacco smoke fogged the room.

"What in the hell is that kid doing here?" someone asked.

"Get outta here, kid," a scantily clad dance hall girl slurred. She had straw-colored hair and curves like nothing the boy had ever seen.

Wade felt his cheeks burn. He shuffled his feet and would have fled back down the stairs had the marshal not set the tumbler aside and raised a hand for silence.

"Do you have a message for me, kid?" Masters asked.

A tremendous wave of relief swept over him, but Wade still took several seconds to find his voice. "Yes, sir, I do."

"Let's hear it." Masters motioned him forward, like a king beckoning a page.

"Sir, it's about the Chambers family." Wade's tongue felt thick in his dry mouth. "I have some information about the murderers."

"Already know all about it," the marshal replied. "It was Injuns."

An angry murmur rippled through the cramped room. Wade shook his head. "No, sir. Indians didn't kill that girl's family at all. The girl, Alice, heard the clicking of stones against horseshoes. 'Like coal miners swinging pickaxes,' that's what she told me. Indians don't shoe their horses. That means someone else—"

Masters grabbed Wade by his lapels and yanked him close. The marshal's face, menacing and repulsive, loomed in Wade's field of vision.

"Let me remind you of something. That girl is not like you and me. She don't talk much because she's feeble-minded."

A belch from the marshal filled the air around Wade's head with the pungent odor of sour mash whiskey. "I happen to know that most of the men who did what they did are long gone. Half of 'em was so drunk, they don't even remember what happened. But folks hereabouts are hot for blood. They ain't gonna rest until they get some vengeance. We're riding out to an Injun encampment at dawn."

"But…" Wade felt so dismayed he grew dizzy.

"You feeble-minded too, little sodbuster? There's no use arguing.

Sometimes this is just how the world works." Masters shoved him away.

Stunned, Wade opened his mouth to speak, thought better of it and took a step back. Like a sleepwalker, he turned and walked stiffly toward the stairs. Laughter and jeers rained down upon his shoulders.

Wade escaped the claustrophobic confines of the upper room and stepped back out onto the stair landing. The night surrounded him, silent and still.

Then he understood. This was just another bad dream. Marshall Masters couldn't be that corrupt, that cruel. The world did not work this way. Wade rejected the notion.

Justice would be served. He had to speak to the marshal—the real marshal.

That meant ending this nightmare, and Wade knew how to wake himself.

He lifted one leg after the other over the landing's wooden guardrail. The boy teetered for a moment, steadying his resolve. Then he pushed off and tumbled into darkness.

ESOTERIC INSURANCE, INC

IT WASN'T LIKE THE OLD DAYS. Not that Obed had actually been around for the "old days," at least how his father described them. The old man loved to talk about how great things were before the Esoteric Order had become incorporated—midnight sacrifices and blood orgies, dark pacts forged on jagged sea cliffs, nights spent swimming deeper and deeper and deeper. Granted, Obed didn't think he'd enjoy a sacrifice, and he didn't really have the stomach for a blood orgy, but anything had to be better than standing in the rain patiently waiting to ruin someone's life.

"It's all right here." The client pressed a loose sheaf of papers into Obed's hands.

He shuffled through the documents, trying not to wince at the client's anxious, yet hopeful smile. The man looked about Obed's age, dark hair flecked with gray, worry lines bunching the corners of his mouth. He probably had a kid in college, maybe two, a car loan, a mortgage on the house that was even now sinking into the muddy ground behind them.

They're not people, they're clients, Obed reminded himself.

The man swallowed. "I bought everything y'all offered: flood, fire, earthquake, burglary—all of it."

"I'm sure you did, Mr. Allen." Obed took a wet, raspy breath, dreading what came next. "Unfortunately, your policy doesn't cover acts of god."

A series of quick-changing emotions swept across Mr. Allen's face: surprise, disbelief, anger. He could've been following a script. "Listen, this is a mudslide or a sinkhole. No god here."

"I'm afraid so." If there was a script, Obed had his part to play, too. "Per the Infinite Fairness in Insurance Act, gods are defined as all beings who exist either all or partly outside time and space." He squatted, pointing at the puddle of viscous slop next to Allen's front porch. "These are clearly dhole excretions. You might know dholes better as chthonians, but either way, as vermiform creations of Shudde M'ell, they're exempt."

The dhole slime was something of a relief, actually. Gods, spirits, and Old Ones were everywhere, but it was seldom this obvious. Last week, Obed had been forced to reach all the way back to Azathoth to find an exception.

"Please! Look again," Allen said.

Obed fixed him with a long stare, sighed, and then riffled through the papers. They both knew it was for show. No matter his car, his house, his life, Mr. Allen hadn't been born with "the look," and that meant he didn't have the coverage, didn't have anything, as a matter-of-fact.

"Everything we had was in there." Allen ran a hand along his stubble, blinking. Now came the client's only real choice: fury or grief. Obed wasn't sure which was worse. "What am I going to tell my family?"

Grief, then.

"Sorry, there's nothing I can do," Obed said. It wasn't *exactly* true. There were loopholes—maddening eccentricities and escape clauses wriggling deep within blocks of cyclopean text. Mr. Allen's mind wasn't equipped to find them; at least if he wanted to keep his sanity, but Obed could—no one knew the rules better than Obed. He could get Mr. Allen his payment, but it would take a night of paperwork. Not to mention it would piss Randy off. Esoteric Insurance's regional manager had been known for his temper even before the change; now that Randy was eight feet tall with claws like fishhooks, Obed was doubly concerned about cutting corners.

He held out the insurance documents. When Mr. Allen didn't take them, he let the papers tumble to the muddy ground.

Mr. Allen slumped back on the crumbling remains of his porch and covered his face with his hands.

Obed almost wished the man would take a swing at him.

Grief is definitely worse.

He walked away, trying to keep his back straight, his shoulders high even though he dearly wanted to drop to all fours and scuttle back to his car. Obed's father might be a relic, but he was right about one thing: this wasn't the old days. Esoteric Insurance was a business now, and in this business, a professional appearance meant everything.

"This isn't right," Mr. Allen called after him.

"I'm sorry, sir. It's the law." Obed turned away, feeling a familiar heaviness settle in his stomach. Nobody ever said the job would be easy. Clients looked at him and they saw a paunchy, sallow-skinned insurance adjuster with no chin and a receding hairline; they didn't see a man with two aging parents to look after, a house, a car, and a life.

His car windows were open, the interior damp with rain, which was nice. At least this had been the last case of the day. He loosened his tie and headed home, wondering if he should get takeout—maybe sushi, or a pizza. Obed's mother wasn't likely to want any, but his father, for all his bragging about cannibalism, would absolutely devour an extra-large anchovy pie.

As he drove, Obed came upon a woman lying in the middle of the road, face down, her arms and legs spread so Obed couldn't tell if she was alive or dead. This happened from time to time, when someone couldn't bear to live any longer or a corpse washed up from the sewers. He wondered if he should stop. Maybe he could talk to her, maybe he could help, or maybe it would be a waste of time.

He checked his mirrors for traffic, then drove around the woman. Someone else would stop. She shifted as he passed, watching him with eyes like bits of wet slate, one hand raised, fingers hooked as if to drag his car closer.

Obed stamped on the gas, accelerating away. A few turns and she was lost from sight. It was sad, he reflected. Sad and unfair. Whatever happened to her wasn't Obed's fault. He was just living his life like everyone else.

He turned on the car radio, tapping his fingers to the tongueless howls of the Easy Listening channel. Still, he couldn't get her face, her *expression* out of his head—hopeless, broken, just like Mr. Allen, just like all of them. Obed ran a hand through his thinning hair. Pizza didn't sound so good anymore.

In fact, he didn't feel hungry at all.

Obed took his time climbing the creaking stairs that led to the Fever Attic, so named because the garish paisley rug and yellow wallpaper reminded him of the frequent fever dreams he'd had as a child. He would've avoided it completely except his mother had shut herself up there months ago after a fight with Obed's father— as if she could lock out both her husband and the change.

Obed skipped a step to avoid a spot he knew creaked and lurched sideways to avoid another squeaky board. He realized his gait resembled a jester's dance and, reminded of Poe's dwarfish Hop-Frog, he flushed and dropped to all fours. Work had his head all turned around; if a man couldn't scuttle in his own home, where *could* he scuttle?

As always, he paused outside the door, not certain if he would feel more relieved if she hadn't changed, or if she *had*.

A blast of hot, dry air met Obed as he slipped into the attic. A row of dehumidifiers lined the far wall, matched by a half-dozen space heaters spread around the room, and still the place was damp, water stains and black mold visible where the yellow wallpaper had peeled away from the ceiling. He wrinkled his nose at the smell of the place.

Obed's mother was in bed, watching him, her eyes narrowed to slits, her lips pressed tight. She'd pulled the blanket up over her legs. Blue veins crisscrossed her skin like rivers on a map, the surrounding flesh luminous in the evening shadows. She laid still, hands resting on her Bible. Obed could see the bloody gashes where she'd cut away the webbing between her fingers again.

She shifted as he entered, the mattress making a wet, sloshing noise. "Obediah."

"Don't call me that."

"It's the name I gave you." His mother gave a phlegmy cough. "Obediah was a prophet in the good book."

"Which one?"

She heaved her great bulk up to glare at him. "This is the time of tribulation John of Patmos prophesied. Abaddon, the angel of death, flies free; the Dragon gathers his loyal followers; the Beasts of the Sea cavort below my window, and yet I am not afraid."

Obed gave her a tired smile. "How do you feel?"

She laid back. "How was work?"

Obed turned away to hide his flush, making a show of checking her breakfast tray. "You're not eating. It's important to keep your strength up."

"Why?"

Obed gripped the tray tight. "The change is an honor, you know."

"That's your dad talking. I won't go down, not now, not ever. I'd rather die and let my spirit fly up to heaven." She paused, regarding him. "Where will you go, Obediah?"

He felt like a pinned insect in a display box whenever his mother watched him like that. "I'll bring you food. Fish if you're up to it, or salt broth, if you'd rather..."

She rolled over, bed creaking. Obed stared at her broad back, shaking his head. Her body, so ungainly on land, would be fast and sleek in the cold dark beneath the waves, and yet she refused, collecting dehumidifiers and space heaters as if they could stop the change.

He chewed his lip. "Mom, you should—"

"How many lives did you ruin today, Obed? How many people did you help kill?"

He turned and hurried across the room.

"'All of us have become unclean, and all our righteous acts are like filthy rags.'" Her words followed him. "'We shrivel like a leaf, and, like the wind, our sins will sweep us—'"

He closed the door.

Downstairs, he grabbed some kelp beer and turned on the news. There was a story about Esoteric Insurance. Nightgaunts had flensed another group of protesters outside the district office. There was a clip of a lawyer-woman, April Derleth, asserting the demonstration had been peaceful; that incorporated cults were contributing to systemic inequalities; that access to food, water, housing, and medicine were basic human rights. She looked familiar, but Obed couldn't place her. The clip cut to a blurry video of a security nightgaunt snatching her up. Obed winced as they flapped off screen and reached for the remote. He already knew how this would end.

There was a splash from the basement.

Obed set his beer down, shaking his head. Dad had flooded the cellar again. He stamped on the floor. When the splashing continued, Obed pushed from his chair to crawl across the house. He opened the basement door, saw what awaited him, and sighed.

Obed's father had plugged up the sump, letting brackish water bubble up through the gravel cellar and into the finished part of the basement. At least he'd remembered to turn the circuits off this time, although it left everything pitch black. Obed used his phone's flashlight app to survey the damage.

Bits of cardboard, ruined clothes, and a few of his mother's keepsake ornaments floated on the filthy water. Obed scowled as one of his old baby albums bobbed by, the pictures all runny and waterlogged.

"Dad!" Obed slapped the surface of the makeshift pond. Ripples spread from his hand, lapping over the top of the washer/dryer—which was probably *also* ruined.

When nothing broke the surface, he stepped into the water, chiding himself for not changing clothes. Another suit ruined.

He could see his father at the far corner of the basement, a pale blur near the workout equipment Obed had bought and never used. At least the water felt nice, a bit warmer than he would've preferred, but not bad.

In the light of the phone, he could just make out his father's features: eyes squeezed shut in concentration, long, greasy hair like loose strands of kelp in the standing water, a thin trickle of bubbles slipping through his pursed lips.

Obed knew it was coming, but still leapt back with a shout when his father surged up, water cascading off his naked form.

"Obediah!" His father blinked the water from his eyes, grinning.

"Don't call me that."

And why not? It's a strong name, an *ancient* name." His father clapped him on the shoulder.

"We talked about this."

"About what?"

"*This*." Obed gestured at the flooded basement. "You know salt water is *murder* on the plumbing."

"I know, I know, but I had to celebrate." His father bared flat, human teeth. "See, they're getting sharper, and look——" He lifted one leg from the water, revealing toes that looked normal apart from a very bad case of fungus. "It's *finally* happening, don't you think?"

"Definitely," Obed lied. He didn't have the heart to tell the truth to a man who had put forty years in with the cult only to be left high and dry with a pension that barely covered utilities. "Now why don't you go upstairs, towel off, and have some fish to celebrate?"

With a nod, his father waded toward the stairs. Shaking his head, Obed followed him upstairs.

Gods, sometimes it felt like he was raising two children.

"So, how many people did you kill today?" his dad asked once Obed had gotten him dried off and into a pair of overalls.

"You know we don't do that anymore."

"Of course, of course. I get it." His father gave him a conspiratorial wink, then leaned in. "C'mon, you can tell me."

"No one. Honestly."

"Oh, come on!"

Obed blew out a long sigh. It was clear his father wasn't going to give up. "Well, two of my clients *did* hang themselves. And there was a woman in the street on the way home."

"My boy!" His dad nudged him in the ribs. "Did you see the news?"

"The protest?"

"You mean the riot?" His dad opened the refrigerator and rattled around, pulling out two kelp beers and a plate of raw fish. "It's these kids. They think the whole world revolves around them. In my day, we'd toss the lot of them off a cliff or cut them open with a kris knife. Gods, remember my old sacrificial dagger? Big ol' gold handle, blade curvy as a slithering snake, rubies in the pommel. Wonder where it got to?"

"It's probably in the basement," Obed said.

"Loved that knife. Always carry a blade, my son. Always," his dad said around a big mouthful of fish. "Back in my day we didn't need security nightgaunts. We would've tickled those protesters ourselves."

"I don't think—"

"They deserved what they got. Shouldn't have resisted."

"That's the thing." Obed winced, thinking of the surprised expression on Derleth's face as the nightgaunt carried her away. "I don't think they did."

There were still smears of blood on the parking lot outside the Esoteric Insurance district office, little bits of hair and gristle baked into the cracks in the asphalt. Obed felt nervous, but the remains weren't the reason why. He'd been called in to meet with the regional manager. Rumor was Randy had contacted corporate HR, which meant things were either very good or very bad.

Caught up in nervous prognostication, Obed nearly drove over the woman. To be fair though, she *was* lying in his parking spot.

He recognized her from the road last night, and from the TV— April Derleth. She wasn't moving, although as Obed threw the car in reverse, he did see her flinch at the noise. The nightgaunt must've dropped her in the housing development and for some reason she'd crawled back here.

Scowling, Obed drove around and parked in a visitor space. This was just what he needed going into a meeting with Randy.

April, *the woman*—Obed knew he shouldn't use her name—made a soft rattling noise as he walked past. He chewed his lip, feeling just like when his mother stared at him.

What did they expect him to do? Quit? Stop paying the mortgage? Put his parents out on the street?

Obed walked past her, his throat hot and tight, the skin between his shoulder blades crawling. He told himself there was nothing he could do. But if that was true, why did he feel so bad?

The EI district office was a ramshackle multi-story building squatting sullenly at the edge of the sea as if it wanted nothing more than to leap from the rocky cliff and into the waves. Inside, a single naked light bulb barely swept back the darkness. The antique security desk was unoccupied.

Obed let his gaze linger on the ancient texts and tomes of unearthly insurance regulations spread across the surface of his desk.

Checking his messages, he saw the meeting was scheduled for the sepulcher, and felt another wave of clammy anxiety wash over him.

A trio of skittering shadows disappeared into holes in the wall as he pushed into the stairwell. He paid them no mind. Instead, he crouched and slid his fingers across the floor until finding the cold iron ring he sought. The trapdoor rose with a bark of protest, and cold dank air rushed up to touch his face. Obed descended into the cool darkness, treading on rustic footholds carved into the stone.

The red exit sign provided barely enough light to see, so Obed flicked his flashlight app on again.

His shoes scraped the gritty sub-basement floor. The meager light revealed a pair of wooden barrels, an empty wine rack, and a few scattered bones of varying sizes and shapes.

In the farthest corner of the room, a crevice gaped like a toothless mouth. Obed lay on his belly and scrabbled through the opening. Another suit ruined, but that was to be expected. The darkness and the tunnel walls pressed in against him. The tunnel was a natural spring, and water trickled between his hands and knees, soaking through his pants.

Obed emerged at the edge of a deep, murky pool. Water dripped from stalactites overhead. About thirty yards away, Obed saw a faint glow beneath the water—sunlight, as seen through the cavern's egress into the sea. The tide was coming back in, and the sepulcher would soon fill to the ceiling. The distant light diminished as a huge shadow shifted in the water.

"*There* he is!" A raspy voice echoed from the darkness off to Obed's left. "This is the guy I've been telling you all about! Best adjuster in the tri-county area!"

Obed turned to see Randy Waites, the regional manager, emerge from the gloom, his smile sharp enough to cut glass. The manager's eyes were a luminous green, his underslung jaw filled with broken-bottle teeth, his legs and arms long and multi-jointed, to better scuttle along the ocean floor.

"And *punctual*, too." Randy slapped Obed on the back, hooked claws digging into his skin.

Obed winced, trying to keep his smile.

"Ah, sorry about that." Randy drew his hand back. "Still getting used to these."

The thing in the pool shifted.

"*Exactly*. So, I was just telling the Ineffable Shadow here about your record. Shadow arrived last night from corporate HR over in Y'ha-nthlei." Randy grinned. "Obed, Shadow. Shadow, Obed."

"Nice to meet you," Obed said.

Motion again from shape in the pool.

"*Exactly*." Randy said. "Obed's closed more cases than anyone in the office, hundreds of clients and not a single payment. No one knows the rules better than this guy does. *No one*. And his suicide percentage is through the roof. The guy's a born killer, a *real* monster."

Obed swallowed. "I don't think—"

"No need to be modest," Randy said. "Here we are, drowning in regulation and every idiot with a cell phone camera acting like an investigative reporter. Not like the old days, eh?"

The thing in the pool shifted.

"*Exactly*." Randy nodded.

Obed took Randy's humor as a good sign. They weren't going to fire him, apparently. But Obed still felt like algae scraped off the bottom of a boat, and he couldn't shake the tightness in his shoulders.

"Ah, well the old days are gone." Randy heaved a wet sigh. "Relics like me don't know how to handle all these social media outlets and class-action lawsuits. That piece on the riot last night was a firestorm. Everyone's emailing, and on the message boards, calling for my resignation."

"Riot?" Obed asked.

"Yeah, last night, a bunch of violent protestors tried to storm the office." Randy winked one bulging eye. "At least that's the story we're pushing."

Bubbles floated to the surface of the pool.

"*Exactly*," Randy said. "So, Obed, you're probably wondering why we called you down here."

"Actually, I—"

"I'm retiring, you see. The powers that be think it's time for EI to embrace the future. No more sacrifice and blood orgies, no more dragging people into the ocean. Our future is about quiet desperation, the slow wear of waves on stone. Madness, hopelessness, driving people to the brink then stepping back and letting them stumble over." Randy spread his webbed fingers. "We need a rules guy, someone with a head for memos and clauses. The numbers say *no one* is better at that than you, and Corporate HR agrees."

The thing in the shallow pool shifted once more.

"*Exactly.*"

Obed felt like he was deep underwater, the entire ocean pressing down on him. He'd just been doing his job, keeping his head down. He'd never even thought to look at his numbers, he'd never thought of himself as a killer, as a monster.

"We want you to take over as regional manager," Randy said. "Get your feet wet. If things go well, you can scuttle on up to corporate. Maybe make director. Who knows? Maybe even make CEO in time."

"This is a lot to process."

"The Ineffable Shadow has already pushed the paperwork through. You're on the fast track, my friend. Here's the company card. Take a few days—swim in the ocean, have some drinks, devour a child. Y'know, *celebrate*."

"Sure, okay." Obed accepted the credit card. "Thank you."

"Get out of here, enjoy yourself." Randy slapped him on the back, then gave an exaggerated wince. "Sorry."

Obed crawled out of the sepulcher, barely aware of the reeking damp. Outside, he sat in his car, windows up, the humidifier blasting. The promotion was everything he thought he'd wanted; everything his dad had worked his whole life for but never gotten. More money, more power, more responsibility.

More responsibility.

There was a soft scratching on his car door. Obed rolled down his window and looked out to see the woman. *April.* She was lying alongside the car, her clothes torn and dirty, one eye swelled shut, her hair matted with blood.

"Shit," Obed said as he opened the door.

"Shit," he repeated as he gingerly picked her up, looking around to make sure no one was watching.

"Shit," he said again as he laid her down in the back seat.

"Shit. Shit. *Shit!*" He drove from the parking lot, still not sure what he would do with the half-dead woman. Eat her. Help her. Take her home. He gulped at that last thought.

Gods, what would his parents think?

Obed carried April into the living room, set her gently on the couch, and climbed to the Fever Attic.

His mother's face conveyed disapproval as he announced his promotion, but he'd expected as much. When he revealed April's presence downstairs, she clawed the air with her hands, as if slicing off his words, and floundered into a sitting position.

"Get her out of the house," she croaked. "Now."

For a moment, Obed could only gape. "But Mom, I thought you, of all people, would feel some compassion."

"Don't be a fool, Obediah! It's a—"

Below, someone screamed.

Obed turned and pounded down the stairs.

He got to the living room in time to see his father looming over the couch. April had curled into a fetal position, one arm thrust out as if to ward off her attacker, whose menacing grin expressed only cruel intentions.

"Dad! What are you doing?"

"Found my dagger. Now we can cut her up proper!" Obed's father straightened, gesturing toward the injured lawyer. "Why else would you bring her here?"

Obed reached out, and for one brief moment, he understood his father. April wasn't a person. If anything, she was prey. The world was cruel, cruel and mad, just like Father Dagon, like all the Elder Gods. Obed was a fool to pretend it was anything else. The powerful—the monsters—did as they wished, and the prey, well, they prayed. It wasn't right, but that didn't matter. And yet, Obed felt something tighten in his chest, a bit of conscience lodged like gristle in his teeth.

He wasn't a monster. At least he hoped he wasn't.

"Stop!" He leaped forward. "Don't!"

His father narrowed his eyes. "Why?"

Obed's mind raced. *Why, indeed?* he thought.

What purpose would his saving April serve? They weren't lovers, or even friends. He was putting his position with Esoteric Insurance in jeopardy. He glanced at April and saw she'd lapsed into unconsciousness. Obed's stomach tightened at the way her bloody hair framed her face, the way she was sprawled on the couch, helpless and hopeless.

"You're not going to touch her, Dad," Obed said.

His father made an irritated sound in the back of his throat. "What do you mean?"

"I didn't bring her home for you to eat," Obed said. "I want to —"

A heavy thump sounded above them. *Gods! If Mom comes down now...*

"What's she up to?" His father looked up as floorboards creaked above Obed's head. "Stay upstairs, Lavernia. This is men's business."

The gurgling roar from upstairs gave Obed the chance to grab April and flee the house.

With April in the back seat of his car, he drove the night streets in an aimless pattern, seeking inspiration. Preoccupied, he almost hit a huge piece of cracked bone in the street. He fought with the steering wheel, jumped the curb, and threw his car into park, his heart pounding.

Obed caught sight of a patrolling nightgaunt and killed the ignition. He followed its soaring arc with his eyes, not daring to move. It made a lazy loop, circling as if it was looking for someone, maybe looking for *him*. Had someone seen him rescue April? When the nightgaunt disappeared behind a building, Obed waited for it to drop onto the hood of his car.

After several minutes, he spotted the nightgaunt fleetingly silhouetted by the moon. It was much smaller, much farther away. Obed turned the keys and eased his car back onto the street as quietly as he could.

He kept to side streets and alleys, scanning the night sky for any sign of pursuit. Though the buildings on either side of the alley seemed to lean toward each other to the point of collapse, Obed still felt exposed and vulnerable. He gazed at April and wondered again why he hadn't just left her alone.

Something touched his arm and Obed lurched away, stifling a cry. His fear lasted only a moment; April's hand wavered midair. He reached back to clasp it, marveling at how soft her skin was. "Hang in there, okay? I'm going to get you to a hospital."

The intake nurse gazed at him with a bland, disconnected expression.

"She's hurt," he announced.

"Put her there, please." The nurse indicated a gurney. Obed lay April softly upon it.

When he returned to the desk, the nurse handed him a thick sheaf of papers on a battered clipboard. "Fill these out."

"Yes, of course." Obed swallowed. "But I'm afraid I don't know much about this woman."

"You know we can't treat someone like her without insurance."

The nurse shrugged. "It's the law."

Five seconds passed, then ten. Obed fumbled for the edge of the counter and gripped it. The intake nurse waited, saying nothing. Another ten seconds passed before he made his decision.

"I, uh..." Obed rooted around in his suit jacket. "I have this." He placed the Esoteric Insurance company credit card on the counter.

"Oh, *Obed*." A familiar voice rasped behind him.

Obed turned to see Randy Waites, followed by a security nightgaunt, wings folded to fit into the reception room. Its featureless face cocked as if testing the air, its claws twitching in anticipation.

His boss shook his head. "Obed, I am *so* disappointed in you."

Obed knuckled a bit of blood from his split lip, glaring across the limo at his father.

The old man didn't meet Obed's gaze. He'd been quiet since the nightgaunt tossed Obed into the limo. A company man to the end.

"I thought you were smarter than this, Obed." Randy lifted April's head. Points of blood marked where his claws dug into her cheeks. She moaned, eyes flickering, but didn't regain consciousness.

"You *had* to know it was a test." Randy let her drop. "Did you think she just *crawled* back to the office?"

Obed felt a flush creep up his neck, but Randy didn't seem to notice. The nightgaunt had insisted on giving Obed a good "tickle" en route to the car, leaving painful cuts on his face and arms. The fact that he hadn't resisted didn't seem to have figured into the creature's consideration.

"I put myself on the line for you," Randy said. "What am I

supposed to tell the Ineffable Shadow? Do you have any idea how long I've been waiting for the stars to align right for me to retire? Now we've got to start the whole thing over again." Randy sat back with a sigh. "There's nothing for it. We'll have to sacrifice both of you."

"That wasn't part of the deal," Obed's father said. "I called you so you *wouldn't* kill him."

"*Someone* needs to appease Father Dagon," Randy said.

"Take me, then."

Randy snorted. "And *that's* why you never made management."

Obed's father looked at his hands as the limo drifted to a stop.

"Ah, here we are." Randy's grin dripped with cruel promise as the doors swung open. He crawled outside, muttering to the guard, "Careful, now. We need them mostly intact."

Either the nightgaunt didn't hear, or didn't care.

The altar had seen better days. Situated on the rocky cliff below the Esoteric Insurance District Office, it had fallen into disuse after the cult incorporated. Now, the slab was chipped and salt-rimed, its sigils almost invisible beneath decades of bird droppings.

This time, Obed *did* try to fight back as the nightgaunt pressed him down on the altar, and earned a few more cuts and bruises for his trouble. It dropped April's limp body on the rock next to him. Obed was relieved to see her chest move with the faintest flutter of breath. Then he remembered where they were and what was about to happen.

"All right, old man." Randy handed Obed's father a curved golden dagger. "Show me I was wrong about you."

It started to rain, big, fat drops that bled through Obed's suit to trace icy lines down his ribs. The nightgaunt's grip was tight on his wrists, its claws sharp as knapped obsidian. Overhead, the clouds darkened, beginning to swirl as if in preparation for a typhoon.

Obed heard the waves crashing on the rocks as his father

trudged forward, long gray hair loose and lank over his face. He held the dagger in trembling hands, lifting the blade gingerly, as if it might bite him.

"Iä Dagon! Iä Hydra! Ineffable Shadow, Lord of the Unfathomable Gulf, Master of Human Resources—we release you from your bonds! Rise and accept this sacrifice!" Randy spread his arms, head tilted back in wild ecstasy as he choked out incantations in the old tongue. Below, the water began to swirl, a blot of darkness growing under the waves. Obed had thought the Ineffable Shadow waited just below the surface, but now he saw it was vast, vast and terrible, free of trivial concepts such as space or distance. It wasn't growing, it was getting closer, and yet, somehow, it had always been there.

"Gods, how I *missed* this." Randy's grin stretched inhumanly wide.

Obed met his father's eyes. The old man raised the dagger, wincing.

"Go on, Dad." Obed didn't look away. "It's what you've always wanted."

"You got me wrong, boy." The reply was soft, almost a whisper.

"Do it!" Randy bellowed, stepping closer. "Before the Shadow swallows us all!"

Obed's father spun, slashing at Randy's throat.

The blade snapped off at the hilt.

Randy squatted to pick up the broken dagger. "It's fake, you idiot. You think I would trust a washed-up old pensioner like you with a *real* blade? I just wanted to see if you'd actually go through with it."

"Don't need your knife, boss." Obed's father said with a tight smile. "A good cultist always brings his own. I just needed to distract you."

Randy cocked his head. "Distract me from wh—"

A dark shape lunged from the boulders to Randy's left, tackling him from the ledge.

"'And lo, the Dragon was hurled down!'" Obed's mother howled as she and Randy tumbled from sight, tearing at each other.

At the same moment, Obed's father drew his old dagger, stepping up to slash his blade across the throat of the nightgaunt holding Obed. The creature tried to turn, but Obed clamped onto its wrists, holding on even though it felt as if the thing would dislocate his arms.

His father stabbed and stabbed, with tenacious persistence, and the nightgaunt's thick, black blood spurted hot against Obed's exposed skin. It struggled soundlessly, slashing at Obed's father with its barbed tail.

"You think I've never been tickled before?" His father laughed as he dragged the blade across the nightgaunt's back, spilling strange organs and viscera onto the rain-slick stone.

At last, the creature went still.

Obed pushed himself up from the slab. Thunder rumbled overhead, flashes of eldritch lightning giving the sky a greenish cast. Tendrils of darkness broke the churning sea, crawling across stone and sand as the Ineffable Shadow crept closer to where Randy and his mother struggled on the rocks below.

Obed's mother was easily twice the size of the regional manager, but her body was better suited to the deeps. Randy scratched at her eyes, his long, fishhook claws cutting deep furrows into her face.

Obed and his father started down the narrow stone steps that led to the rocks, taking them two at a time. They reached the outcrop in time to see Randy slam Obed's mother to the stone, his eyes glowing a furious green in the storm-lit gloom.

Obed's father ran at Randy with the dagger. Randy slapped him aside with almost casual ease, then spun toward Obed, claws flexing. "C'mon! You wanna take a swing at the champ?"

Obed eyed his boss. Even uninjured he wouldn't have fancied his chances against Randy. The man was monstrous, a relic from when Esoteric Insurance had been an Eldritch cult run by murder and rites, not memos and rules. But times had changed—and *no one* knew the rules better than Obed.

"Stop. Just, stop." He held up a hand. "You're embarrassing yourself."

"What?" Randy growled.

"Gods, where do I start? Misappropriation of company resources, abducting an EI employee, improper use of a company vehicle, unlicensed sacrifice." Obed ticked them off on his fingers, and then nodded at the Ineffable Shadow. "Not to mention you didn't file *any* of the proper paperwork for a summoning."

"That's ridiculous, I—"

Obed shouted over him. "Company bylaws require you go on unpaid leave pending a full inquiry."

"I'll rip your pudgy little—" Randy paused, glancing down at the shadow that had swallowed his legs. He looked up, lantern-bright eyes wide with panic.

"Guess the Ineffable Shadow agrees with me." Obed grinned. "It is with HR, after all."

In another moment, Randy was gone.

Obed and his parents made their way back to the ledge, leaning on each other for support. He knelt to slip aching arms under April, tottering like a newborn colt as he stood, a fishhook of pain lancing through his side with each labored breath. It was worth it when she curled close, her face pressed to his chest as if she knew she was finally safe.

"Guess I should start looking for a new job," Obed said as they began the long, slow climb back to the parking lot. "I don't think corporate is going to want me for regional manager anymore."

"Don't be so sure," his father said. "Killing the previous manager is company tradition. How do you think Randy got his job?"

"'And so did the whole world come to worship the Beast Out of the Sea.'" His mother panted as if in pain. Fortunately, her eldritch biology already seemed to be closing the slashes Randy had left in her sides. "'But the people asked, "Who is like the beast? Who can wage war against it?"'"

His father snorted.

"Enough." Obed shook his head. "We'll talk about this when we get home."

His parents glared at each other.

Gods, sometimes it was as if he was raising two children.

An eruption of flowers brightened the room. Cards piled on the nightstand. April lay in bed. Monitors and IV drips beeped cheerily in the morning light.

Obed set his flowers with the others and turned to see April watching him. She wasn't smiling. For a moment, Obed felt confused, until he realized this was the first time they'd met when she was *actually* conscious.

"I'm Obed," he said.

"Ah." She gave a tight smile. "They say you brought me in."

"Yes, that and—" he frowned, trying to find the right words. "There were nightgaunts, and a sacrifice, and crawling darkness, and my mom and dad, and well—" He swallowed. "I was wondering if we could talk about it all over dinner."

She cocked her head, frowning. "I don't think that would be appropriate."

"What?"

"You're the regional manager at Esoteric Insurance, right?"

Obed didn't trust his voice not to break, so he just nodded.

"Then you should know I'm suing your company for six-hundred million dollars in damages, public endangerment, wrongful death. The list goes on."

"Well, yes, but I thought we might—"

"Listen." She pushed herself up on her elbows. "I'm grateful you brought me in, but it doesn't change who you are or *what* you do."

"But that's not true. I'm going to change the company from within—raise the payout rates, clear up murky clauses, start an outreach program, hire more humans. It could take a while, but I'm working to—"

"People are dying right now."

"What do you mean?"

"Right now, out there." She nodded at the window. "People are dying because of EI."

Obed took a step back. This wasn't going as he'd planned at all.

"I saw you drive by me on the street, walk past me in the parking lot. Does the fact you *finally* did the right thing wipe all that away?"

"But, I—" Obed chewed his lip. She was right.

"And I'm not going to even ask what you think *this* is." April waved a hand between the two of them.

He held up his hands. "I should go."

She sighed. "So that's it? You just going to scuttle back to your job to ruin more people's lives? You've seen what it's like. You *know*."

Obed swallowed. He was regional manager now, with all the benefits and responsibilities.

Responsibilities.

"I know," he said after a moment.

"Then don't forget."

Obed nodded and left the room. He pressed the elevator button, waiting as the numbers on the display blinked upwards. The old days were gone, but after seeing how Randy, his father, even his mother acted, how they lied to themselves, Obed wasn't sure that was a bad thing. It didn't matter if he was the regional manager or a low-level insurance adjustor, he couldn't hide anymore. All his old justifications fell away—to see the people EI hurt, to realize the part he'd played in it, and go back to pretending it wasn't his fault—

Then Obed really would be a monster.

Written in collaboration with Evan Dicken

THE BURIAL SHROUD

MANKIND embraced hatred,
welcomed death's dark abyss.
This time the ovens spared
only the brightest and the best.

THEY burned teachers, preachers, pilots, doctors,
veterans, vegans, peaceniks, and warmongers.
Suicidal, teen idols, both white- and blue-collar,
rich athletes and the bum who wanted a dollar.
Workaholics, alcoholics, nature photographers,
dancers, artists, prisoners, and pornographers.
Skinheads, slumlords, activists, feminists
Muslims, Buddhists, Christians, atheists.

WITH the refinement completed,
the one percent thought they'd won.
Until the ashes of the ninety-nine
rose and blotted out the sun.

SNOW FLIES

THE BITTER JANUARY AIR tormented him, so Gus Griffith tormented the air right back with his singing. His voice sounded like a wagon axel badly in need of greasing.

The afternoon had turned frigid and steely by the time Gus departed Cheyenne and pointed his horse toward home. The blue dun trotted across the frozen prairie, following a trail that led eastward across Wyoming Territory.

Gus' mood had turned ugly. That morning, Maggie's sharp-tongued nagging had motivated him into taking a winter ride. She reminded him that their son, Oren, was due for a horse of his own. Oren had just turned twelve and Gus expected him to complete his fair share of the chores. Maggie reminded him tartly that Oren couldn't accomplish all they expected of him on foot. In the end, Gus had braved the bitter cold just for the change in scenery. He had ridden into town to attend a horse sale and had spent the mid-morning hours surrounded by cattle barons as crooked as a dog's hind legs. Gus had placed a bid here and there, but he lasted about as long as a shot of whiskey in a high-stakes poker game. All the horseflesh rose above any amount he felt willing to pay within two or three bids.

"What kind of horse do you think he's bringing for me, Ma?" Oren fidgeted with excitement.

"I couldn't say. With your father, there's no telling." Maggie stirred the turnip and carrot soup bubbling in the pot. She didn't voice her misgivings about the state in which Gus had left them that morning. Better to focus on dinner than to speculate on her husband's mood. Like a January day, he could remain cold, or surprise her with sunshine.

The sky overhead loomed cloudless, and for that, at least, Gus felt thankful. The sun, descending at his back, provided little warmth, but supplied some light at least. He knew several days could pass before that cheery orb might peep through the winter clouds again.

Best to reach the home place before any snow flies...

Before he finished his thought, Gus cast a suspicious look back in the direction he had come. The sky remained clear. The trick, according to the wizened old man who lived near Sulfur Creek, was not to think about them. *Good advice.*

Factoring in the wind chill, Gus knew it had to be colder than twenty degrees below zero, though he did not know the exact temperature. He hoped to reach home before dark, but cursed himself for stopping first for a drink at the Mint Bar.

The service there was slow as frozen molasses, but the idea of fortifying himself for the bitter ride home had seemed like a first-rate idea at the time. Now he admitted his folly. If he had drunk just one, that might have been all right. But he had needed to dampen the sizzling irritation he felt at coming back from the horse sale empty-handed. He'd had his eye on a good-tempered bay, but a feller built like a rain barrel had waved a hand and bid far more than Gus could afford to pay. So, his single whiskey shot became three... or four. *Five, at most.*

Scowling, Gus urged his horse into a canter. He plunged in among a stand of scrubby, wind-blown ponderosa pines. The trail was faint, and he felt glad he still had light.

His beard and mustache had frosted, the ice increasing with each exhalation. Gus chewed tobacco, and the muzzle of ice held to his lips so firmly that he could not clear his chin when he expelled the juice. The result was a crystallized beard the color of amber increasing in length by minute increments down his chin.

If I fell off my horse, would my beard shatter like a pane of glass?

"I bet he gets me a strawberry roan." Oren had swept the cabin's floor and now stood gazing out the frosted-over glass pane. "Or a paint! They make good roping horses." He turned toward his mother and grinned.

Maggie seated herself and picked up her sewing. Gus had torn a pair of his heavy wool pants, and she wanted to surprise him by repairing them while he was away. "Whatever he chooses, you just make sure you show your gratitude."

The furrow of the trail sat visible, but the wind had blown snow in small drifts across it, obscuring the hoof prints from his trip into town. He kept urging the dun doggedly onward. Gus remained observant. He didn't dare push his horse too hard, but the longer they remained unsheltered the more their danger increased.

At half-past the hour, Gus arrived at Crow Creek. He felt pleased at the speed he had made. If he kept it up, he would reach the homestead by seven. Gus noted the stinging in his toes and dismounted. Holding the reins, he stamped his feet to restore circulation. Then he walked ahead of the dun, leading it along the creek bank. He searched for a solid path across. He didn't want to ride across the same place they'd crossed this morning. He'd heard the ice crack beneath them, and even hours later didn't feel like tempting fate.

The cold was brutal, unrelenting. It seemed to penetrate his flesh and caress his bones. Gus shivered and beat his hands against his legs. He squinted, considering Crow Creek again. The narrowest place to cross might not be the safest. Should he try to find a deeper portion of the creek where the ice on top might be thicker? On the other hand, maybe they should cross where he knew the creek to be shallow. The whiskey muddled his thoughts, made him feeble north of his ears. *Ride or walk across the ice?* Gus uttered an oath.

The longer he took to decide, the colder his extremities became. At last, with the icy wind biting at his exposed skin, he grabbed the reins and led the dun out onto the ice. Foot by foot, step by tentative step, they made their way across. Each time Gus looked up at the opposite bank, it seemed no closer. He expected the dreaded sound of cracking ice at any moment, but none came, and at last, they made it to safety.

"You need me to break more icicles off the roof to add to the soup water, Ma?"

"No, we should have enough. The water just started simmering." Maggie suspected the boy was searching for an excuse to bundle up and head outside, as if that might somehow hasten his father's arrival. "But if you could snare us a rabbit, we could make a stew," she added wryly.

Oren, she saw, had turned his attention back out the window.

"An appaloosa, I bet." he murmured. "They're good roping horses too. Maybe I ought to start thinking about a name."

They climbed the steep bank and at the top, Gus pushed one booted foot into the stirrup, grabbed hold of the saddle horn and swung his leg over the saddle. He urged his horse into a canter, and then, catching sight of the trail, he raked his spurs into its flanks until the horse leaned into a gallop. Despite the harsh wind and bitter cold, Gus felt good. There'd be another horse sale in the spring. Oren could wait until then. He'd be home soon enough. The family would be there, a fire lit and roaring, and a hot supper bubbling in the pot. Maggie had a tongue like a hickory switch, but she cooked up meals that made his mouth water. Moreover, though he didn't feel comfortable telling her so, he found his wife to be prettier than a pasque flower. *And sweet as wild honey.*

Gus was grinning like a jackass when it happened. At a place where he saw no signs, where the unbroken snow seemed to promise solidness beneath, his horse lurched and stumbled. Gus pitched over the dun's head and the reins tore from his hands. He flew through the air as graceless as a one-winged goose and hit the frozen earth with a teeth-rattling impact.

For several seconds, a black expanse replaced the omnipresence of white.

Gus lay on the frozen ground. He watched in fascination as a pair of horses staggered upright, each holding a foreleg raised gingerly off the ground. He sat up and waited until the two horses merged into one.

Angry and embarrassed, Gus cursed his bad luck. The dun had broken a leg. He could see it lifting a foreleg off the ground. He reached for his felt stockman's hat and bit back a scream of pain. Looking down at his left shoulder, he saw that his entire arm was out of true. *Is it out of its socket?* That seemed the likeliest answer. Gus reached across with his right hand and made a tentative exploration of his injured limb. He knew he had to address one problem at a time, or risk being overwhelmed. He had his shoulder tend to, then his horse, all while staying warm until he could either build a fire or find the trail home. *I sure as hell don't want to be caught in a blizzard of...*

His mind recoiled at the thought. To distract himself, he lifted his good arm, and felt his ice encrusted tobacco juice beard. His hand met with solidity. *By the Lord, how did I bust my shoulder, but my beard is still a damned ice block?*

He knew what he had to do and thought he might end up wringing the whiskey out of his belly in the process. He steadied his breathing and sent up a quick, but heartfelt prayer for courage and strength. Then he threw himself backward against the frozen earth. A tornado of pain howled through the nerves in his shoulder and down his arm upon impact. Gus loosed a torrent of words that would've made a contentious card game between gamblers and outlaws sound like a prayer meeting. Then he sat up fast, scrambled to his knees, and cupped his good hand around the protruding upper part of his injured arm. He pitched forward before he could hesitate. This time he struck the ground with his good elbow first, and with more control. His right hand popped his dislocation back into place.

The muscles in his stomach clenched up and Gus and the Mint Bar's whiskey parted ways. He rolled over onto his back, panting. Gus felt the sheen of sweat on his forehead and the tears on his cheeks freeze in a matter of seconds. This pressed him into action.

Though his shoulder ached something fierce, he had to move, or risk freezing to death—or worse. He rose to his feet, keeping his aching arm close to his side. *Maybe the cold will numb the pain.* He crouched to retrieve his hat and pulled it down over his stinging ears.

His horse stood ten yards from him, still favoring its broken leg. *Must have been a prairie dog hole,* Gus thought. *To blazes with every blasted one of them between here and the Mississippi.* A dawning realization came to him then. If he hadn't been so mulish and had kept bidding, he'd have an extra horse to ride home. Now he had nothing. Gus ground his teeth.

Already responsiveness had gone out of his feet. He hobbled toward his horse, murmuring nonsense words meant to reassure. The blue dun neighed and tossed its head. Its dark mane whipped in the artic-temperature wind. Gus reached out and grasped the dangling reins with his good hand. Now came the tricky part. He didn't carry a six-shooter, so he had to get his hunting rifle out of the scabbard. He had to load it, aim it, and put the dun out of its misery—all with one arm. Then he had to figure out how to travel the last few miles home on foot, and in the dark, without getting lost or freezing to death. All of it added up to a near insurmountable task, but Gus was no tenderfoot. He had grit, and he'd survive, even if he lost a few fingers and toes.

He dropped the reins and reached for the rifle, still encased in its leather scabbard. He pulled it free. It was an old .44 caliber breech-loading Henry rifle. It operated with a lever action, and Gus knew he'd need to make damned sure he made his first shot count. If he botched it, his act of mercy could prove to be an act of futility. He envisioned having to lay it on the ground to work the lever and shook his head in irritation. He wondered if his old horse was worth the effort.

Gus had to look at the rifle to confirm whether he still had hold of it. The telegraph wires connecting his brain and his fingers seemed to be down. He knelt, set the rifle down between his legs, and reached into the pocket where he kept the shells. He withdrew his hand and removed his glove with his teeth out of necessity. He needed to load at least one shell into the magazine, but his fingers had gone numb, and they wouldn't bend. The glove fell from his mouth, into the snow.

He thought he heard an ominous hissing then, and whipped his head around. He saw nothing amiss, no approaching cloud, nor any further indication of impending disaster. Gus paused to make sure. A vision of the toothless old man's grim visage and bleak warnings came into his mind. He wished the Sulfur Creek hermit had never infected him with his crazy notions.

Gus resumed his attempts at retrieving a shell from his pocket. He succeeded, but the shell slipped from his senseless fingers and tumbled into the snow as he tried to lift it. Gus uttered another oath and reached in his pocket for a second shell. He knew they were there because he could hear them clinking and clacking together as he fumbled for one. Try as he would, he could not seize hold of another one, however.

The entire time, in his subconscious, lurked the knowledge that at any moment a telltale white cloud might roil on the horizon. These thoughts tended to put him in a panic, but he fought against them and remained calm.

Gus started to feel better. That's when he realized he was in grave danger. Too much time has passed. He'd lost his battle with the frost. It crept into his body from all sides. He looked down at his feet, but like his fingers, could no longer feel them.

The sun had set, and the sky overhead had darkened. He had to get moving. *To hell with it. I tried.* Let the horse fend for itself. Once he got his blood circulating again, it wouldn't be so bad. He thought walking might even save him from freezing to death.

Gus threw the rifle down and said farewell to his horse by cursing the blue dun's lineage back seven generations. He'd hobbled a dozen steps when his horse lowered his foreleg. Gus stopped.

The horse took a step.

Gus squinted, looking hard at its forelegs, searching for any specific sign of injury.

The horse took another step.

Oh, you damn, dirty skunk. Gus lunged, but the blue dun trotted out of his reach with ease. It tossed its head, whinnied, and trotted away down the trail.

The certainty of death, thorny and oppressive, came over him. The thought of dying far from home and the image of coyotes tearing open his white belly and feasting on his bloody innards threw him into a panic. He turned and broke into a shambling run. He ran blindly, without a plan, not even keeping to the trail. As he plowed and floundered through the snow, Gus despaired. He lamented not spending money on a horse for Oren. What good were his coins now?

Perhaps if he ran on his feet would thaw. He might get within hailing distance of the homestead. It struck him as curious that he could run at all on feet he could not feel. He looked down just to make sure they struck the earth with each bound.

Then his lungs betrayed him. His gasping, panting breaths finally fractured in the cold, and a coughing fit forced him to stop and rest. He thought about building a fire. Gus looked around; saw nothing but snow, and the last spark of hope left him. Gus sank to his knees and then sprawled out on the frozen ground.

Gus let his mind go blank. He drowsed off into what he hoped would be the most comfortable and satisfying rest he had ever known.

"Ma! I see it!" In his excitement, Oren hopped from one foot to the other. "It just crested the hill!"

Maggie rose and joined her son at the window. The bitter cold had covered most of the glass with frost, but Oren cleared a spot with his palm again so they both could see. She stooped behind him and looked over his shoulder.

"There it is, Ma! My new horse is... a blue dun!" Oren narrowed his eyes and frowned. "But that looks like..."

All of a sudden, Maggie felt dreadfully cold.

Oren looked back at the horse approaching through the snow and repeated the words, much quieter this time. "My new horse is a blue dun."

At that same moment, less than a mile away, Gus felt the searing pain of the first sting. He looked down at his frozen hand, hanging from his coat sleeve. An extraordinarily fluffy snowflake had fallen on it. As he looked, the snowflake took flight. It measured over one inch long, and as it darted away on iridescent wings, Gus's breath hitched. He fancied he saw himself reflected in the silvery orbs that comprised its eyes. One hundred distorted mirror images of his face, ice-encrusted mouth dropped open in dismay. The others approached him in a roiling cloud.

Gus knew then with certainty there would be no return home, no joyful family reunion, no welcoming fire. The frigid air resonated with an infernal buzzing. Not wanting to see, he turned anyway to face the oncoming white cloud hell-bent on his destruction.

Like the locusts that plagued the ancient Egyptians, this evolutionary aberration wreaked havoc on every living thing caught in its path. Snow flies were the stuff of nightmares in the colder climates.

The white, buzzing blizzard neared. The insects swarmed above and around him. Searing pain pierced the area of exposed skin between his eyebrows, and his left cheek above his beard. Gus swatted his face with his good hand, not feeling the blow he delivered upon himself. He saw the beating of iridescent wings; transparent, icicle-like proboscis slicing through his clothing; and hairy legs that looked like tendrils of frost. He made one final effort, rose, and shambled three panicked steps before collapsing in the snow. The horde of insects attacked him again and again in a relentless frenzy.

Gus bellowed in pain as each sting cut opened flesh, letting his blood flow. The tissue around each bite reacted as if frostbitten. It would necrotize in minutes, Gus knew, and he would lose all his fingers and most of his face before death took him. He took a measure of solace, knowing the subzero cold would help shorten his suffering.

Writhing in the throes of anguish, his leather pouch fell into the snow. Coins spilled out and scattered across the ground. Gus loosed one final wail of impotent fury, and then disappeared beneath an unrelenting blizzard of white.

THE HORLA RETURNS

"YOU WANTED TO SEE ME, Mr. President?" H.R. Haldeman spoke from the double door entrance to the Oval Office.

Richard M. Nixon looked up from a sheaf of hand-written pages spread out on his mahogany desk and motioned for his chief of staff to be seated.

"It's just you and me, Bob, so let's not stand on formality."

"All right, sir." Haldeman let his gaze linger on his boss' face. Purple crescents hung under the president's eyes. Nixon's face was pale, making his five o'clock shadow even more pronounced.

"You want a drink, Bob? Coffee? Something stronger?"

Haldeman shook his head as he seated himself. He glanced at the papers Nixon kept nervously shuffling beneath his well-manicured fingers.

"This isn't about McGovern, is it? Because his run won't amount to anything. All our straw polls come out overwhelmingly in your favor."

Nixon fixed him with an unhappy expression. "It's not about McGovern, the Democrats, or even China. This is something bigger."

Haldeman felt his eyebrows lift. He extended his hand, indicating the pages. "May I?"

Nixon nodded. Haldeman took the sheets and sat back. He squinted at the slanted, cramped cursive, and read:

John-Albert Hornstra
Rural Route 3
Niobrara, Neb.
68760

April 12, 1972

President Richard Nixon
c/o The White House
1600 Pennsylvania Avenue
Washington, D.C.
20500

Dear Mr. President,

I hope this letter reaches you. I got this address from the public library in town.

I know soon you will be busy campaigning for reelection. I hope I haven't waited too long to write. I am asking for your help.

I am ill and horribly feverish, but I ain't crazy. I live in constant fear of losing my mind, or worse. I work my fields from sunrise to sunset—growing corn, soybeans, and milo this crop rotation—and that gives me something to distract my mind. The fears come on strong at sundown, though. I read from the Good Book and pray a lot, but between you and me, Mr. President, that hasn't been giving me much comfort.

Something fell from the sky one night. I was sitting on the porch enjoying the cool night air and saw it come. Green flames, it had, trailing off behind it. Followed it with my eye and figured it landed somewhere on the other side of the shelter belt of trees that grows on the far side of the nearest gravel road. Guessed it was a meteorite. I grabbed a fire extinguisher and a flashlight from the house and took a hike.

I was disappointed by what I found—or didn't find. Not much of anything really. A groove in the soil about twenty feet long was all. Some of the cornstalks were scorched a bit, but that was it.

Something must have followed me back home, though. Every night, for a week or two after that, whenever I went to bed something would visit me in the early hours of the morning. I felt it drawing near, climbing—or *sliming*—onto my bed. Sometimes it sat on my chest, making it hard for me to breathe. Other times it slithered around my neck and pulled itself tight. Sometimes it flattened itself across my face like a wet towel. I wanted to scream, thrash, and get away, but I couldn't. I just lay there rigid. Frozen. Like how you can't move in a nightmare, except I knew I was awake.

I understand now that it was conducting simple experiments to find out how long I could survive without oxygen. One night, the damned thing slithered right into my mouth and down my throat. My eyes watered. The room spun as I grew dizzy. I felt as if I was suffocating—probably, I was. And then I felt it in my lungs, like thick cigar smoke. It burned at first, but I couldn't summon up a cough. Before long, the unpleasant feeling sort of faded away. I either passed out or slipped into a stupor so deep that I didn't mind this alien incursion.

Now I have a parasite living inside me, like a leech or a tapeworm. Takes part of the air that I breathe, takes sustenance from the food that I eat and the water that I drink.

When I was younger, I read a story about a man who lost himself—mind, body, and soul—to a mysterious, unseen invader. *The Horla*, the author called it. Roughly translates to 'the Outsider' according to the woman who translated the story from French to English. How appropriate. That's an appropriate description of my unwelcome guest.

This creature came from space. I'm convinced of that. But what is it, this unseen being? Is it an 'advance man' sent here to spy on humanity on behalf of an interstellar race?

If I could go far, far away and never return, I might be saved. But that's selfish and short-sighted. Maybe I need to go far, far away so that *everyone else* might be saved.

Mr. President, I know about Area 51, and the grays. I have read extensively and understand the grays were not the real invaders. They were like horses ridden by scouts. It was what was *inside* the grays that humanity should fear. And I believe one of these very same beings is living inside me, now, as I write this.

Every night I lay in the tall grass and gaze up at

the sky. Who inhabits those twinkling worlds? What forms, what living beings, what creatures are there? Do those who have the capability to think on those distant worlds know more than we do? Can we even fathom concepts that are commonplace to them? What do they perceive that we do not? Humanity is warlike; what if these creatures are as well? How soon before they invade our planet? How quickly and easily will humanity be conquered?

What if we are weak, powerless, ignorant, and ripe for conquest? What good are missiles and tanks when our enemy can invade our very bodies?

Mankind has been taking baby steps, and America is leading the way. I have a proposal, Mr. President. I've been following the Apollo moon missions with great interest. My idea is simple. Send me to the moon. Leave me there. I will perish, as will this thing inside me. If there is communication with its own kind, they will receive word of an inhospitable and desolate land. Earth, and all its resources, will be overlooked. This is my sincere hope.

I know if anyone can facilitate this, you can.

I look forward to your reply.

Respectfully yours,
John-Albert Hornstra"

Haldeman read the letter twice. Then he sat and silently reflected. At last, he looked up at his boss. "This isn't your garden variety crackpot, is it?"

The president looked worse than when Haldeman had first

entered the Oval Office. "Bob, you were in the room when we received the briefings about Roswell. He has the details right. He even knows their code name. That's classified, for God's sake!"

"I think that was just a fluke," Haldeman said. He happened to read that old story, that's all. It's his best—or only—point of reference."

"This is a headache. If he goes to the press…"

"He'll get laughed out of the room." Haldeman placed the pages on the desk. "If he goes to one of the gossip rags, we discredit him. Easy."

Nixon slouched and frowned, which added unflattering emphasis to his jowly cheeks. "I'm going to contact Hoover directly. Have him send someone to bring this Hornstra fellow into custody."

Haldeman straightened. "You're not seriously considering sending him to the moon, are you?"

"One step at a time, Bob. One step at a time."

Apollo 17 was the final Moon landing mission of NASA's Apollo program. Its crew consisted of Commander Eugene Cernan, Lunar Module Pilot Harrison Schmitt, and Command Module Pilot Ronald Evans. It also carried a biological experiment, purportedly involving five mice. The astronauts also left seismic explosive charges, which they detonated remotely after leaving the moon's surface. The mission began on December 7 and ended on December 19, 1972.

Humans have not returned to the moon's surface since.

John-Albert Hornstra stood alone in the Camelot Crater and watched as the lunar module lifted off the moon's surface. Cernan and Schmitt would rendezvous and dock with the lunar orbiter. Once the astronauts transferred their equipment and lunar samples, they'd jettison the lunar landing module and begin their journey back to Earth.

He had plenty of time to reflect.

I have done my part, sacrificed my life for the good of all mankind. The alien presence will not infiltrate earth, will not conquer it. Humanity will be free. And when they detonate, the Horla will be destroyed. I will be at peace at last.

John-Albert frowned. *Something isn't right.* The sensation of insidious oppression, the constant corrupt sense of being violated and manipulated—had disappeared. He searched his thoughts; he was alone. The invasive species had departed. But that meant...

John-Albert gazed at the blue and green marble he'd forever left behind. The moon's rotation would soon obscure it from his view. The tiny shape he saw was longer his home. He puzzled over it. He'd felt the Horla's presence during launch, and during the surreal previous days as he dutifully followed the astronauts while they collected their samples and conducted their experiments.

But at some point, the Horla—the Outsider—had left him. John-Albert felt sick. It had known somehow, had seen through the ruse and found a new host. At this moment, the loathsome forerunner of invasion was returning to Earth.

Everything he feared, everything he'd sought to delay or avoid completely could still happen—and likely would. John-Albert considered the extraordinary measures President Nixon had taken, the remarkable cooperation on NASA's part, and those individuals in the military and government who had performed their various duties and honored the secrecy and integrity of the mission.

John-Albert gazed at Earth until it disappeared from his view. He'd long lost sight of the lunar orbiter.

Nearly four billion people living on the planet, and he had failed them.

He was going to die alone, in the bleakest sense of the word.

The tables have turned, he thought. *I am no longer a part of humanity because I am* apart *from humanity. I am the outsider now. I am* the Horla.

INSOMNIA

"I'M SCARED YOU'RE GOING TO leave me when we're older," my wife admits. She is restless beneath the rumpled covers.

"I'm worried you'll try to kill me someday to keep that from happening," I reply.

She doesn't say anything. The breeze hisses at us from outside our window.

"Better check on him," my wife says. I fumble with the covers and trudge across the hall.

The boy has put a makeshift tent up in the spare room. He has chosen to sleep in it. I get down on all fours and crawl in beside him. For a moment, I am convinced he has stopped breathing. I hold my own breath until I hear the air whistling out through his nose. I back out of the tent.

For a moment, I think I see a face through the window, peering in from outside the house. I squint into the darkness but see only the leaves of the shrubbery bobbing in the breeze.

I return to bed. My wife stares at the ceiling, not speaking. I crack my knuckles one by one. Lightning flashes in the distance. No thunder yet.

An intermingling of bleach and something else I don't want to think about burns my nose. I ask my wife if she smells anything unpleasant.

"Did you rinse the bathtub?" she asks. I toss the covers aside. In the bathroom, I run hot water down the drain. It still runs sluggish, clotted with hair and tissue.

"I used a bottle of clog remover," I complain when I'm back in our bedroom. "And it's still draining slow."

"Better check on him," my wife suggests.

Back inside the tent, I touch the boy's cheek. He sits up, rubs his eyes, and stares at me with mistrust. I exit the tent without a word.

I detour to the back door. Someone left it unlocked, so I lock it. After I cross the room, I stand on the landing, gazing down the stairs into the darkened basement. Could someone have entered? Are they waiting down there in the darkness?

I plod through the kitchen, creak down the hall, and grunt into bed. Lightning illuminates the room and thunder growls in the night. I try to crack my knuckles again but only get results from two fingers this time. I grind my teeth instead.

My wife is fitful, cannot keep still. "Better check on him," she says again. I'm halfway out of bed before she's finished speaking.

The boy is still breathing. Outside are only shrubs. The side door remains locked.

I collapse on top of the covers. Deep inhalations from the shape beside me indicate my wife has abandoned me. Now I am alone to stand watch against the night.

We snatched his sister, too, but my wife decided she only wanted to keep the boy.

I grind my teeth and listen to the rain.

PETE GETS OFF THE FENCE

PETE SPENT HIS DAYS WANDERING the wintry streets of Chicago. His dwindling faith in humanity trailed behind him in dispirited fashion, as if tethered by a ghostly filament. He wondered how to strengthen it. The state of the world had him longing for days long passed.

Back then, just when the proverbial night seemed darkest, a hero rose to pierce that darkness. Pete, not content to sit idly by, had chosen to march at the newcomer's side. In fact, he considered himself the hero's right hand man. However, when it mattered most, he let pride and insecurity dictate his actions, and Pete had screwed everything up. He still felt the sharp pang of guilt after all these years.

Everything had gone wrong, yes, but events had ended with a sliver of hope, a lining of silver etched on the dark cloud of history. Rumors of his humiliating, agonizing death spread. As years passed, repeated telling transformed these rumors into facts.

Pete drifted.

Now, many years later and half a world away, each new day brought with it more dispiriting news. Pete wondered why he kept living. Was it his punishment? A mistake? A miracle?

"Come, let us reason together."

Pete paused with his steaming Americano poised an inch from his lips. He glanced around the coffee shop to determine who had spoken.

"You know better than that," the disembodied voice said.

Pete redirected his gaze out the window. Across the busy street, a gaunt-cheeked figure hunched against the Chicago wind. His skin was as dark as Pete's, and his wiry gray beard and shoulder-length hair whipped like shrubbery in a hurricane. His sunken eyes hid in pockets of shadow. He spoke again, though his lips did not move.

"Be a pal, huh? Don't leave me hanging."

"That's in very poor taste," Pete muttered, shaking his head in disbelief. He had not expected to see this one ever again, but there he stood. Pete set his drink down and shoved his chair back from the table.

Outside, the bitter wind blowing in off Lake Michigan buffeted Pete's frame as he trudged across the street. He approached the spot where the hunched figure had stood. Bundled pedestrians hurried past him, but he saw no sign of the man. The skin on his neck prickled in warning and he turned. Though his vision blurred in the stinging cold, Pete watched the man who had lured him outside take his seat at the coffee shop table. The man raised his coffee cup as if in toast, grinned through the glass, and drank.

I'm not ready for this. Pete stuffed his hands in his pockets and hurried away up the street.

"Pete and Repeat sat on a fence!" A bedraggled figure called to him from a brownstone's stoop. "Have a seat and let's settle this."

For a fleeting moment, Pete considered running away. He recognized the man who had stolen his seat, and drink, at the coffee shop three days earlier. Pete thought he recognized sorrow, warmth, and perhaps even madness intermingled in the other man's eyes.

"You trying to give me a heart attack?" Pete scowled and tried to lend some gravel to his voice. "What do you want?"

The other man's shoulders sagged. "Don't be that way. The time has come for us to talk of many things."

"Like what?" Pete scoffed. "Cabbages and kings? It's already been done." He shoved his hands in his pockets and hurried away. As he crossed the next intersection, he listened for any indication the man had followed him, but heard nothing. Pete hazarded a quick glance behind him.

"I'm right here." Pete spun around. The man waited on the far side of the street, ahead of him. *Tricky*, Pete thought. *He let me leave last time. This time, he won't.* The shabbily dressed man fell into step beside Pete. As they passed the mouth of an alley, he motioned toward an overflowing dumpster. "Let us look upon the detritus of a departed soul."

With a sigh of resignation, Pete shuffled forward, and scanned the scattered bags and jumbled boxes. These were the earthly remains of someone who had lived in squalor, yet had no shortage of material possessions.

His companion fished a hand inside one of the boxes. A sad smile transformed his features as he withdrew a votive candle. The scarred hand disappeared again and withdrew a reading lamp with a grooved, flexible neck. Pete glanced in and saw lamps and lights of all shapes and sizes. "She feared the darkness," his companion said. "Kept every light burning, even when she took her rest." Pete tried to identify the other man's emotions as he spoke. *Melancholy? Regret?*

"She needn't have been fearful of darkness. In and of itself, darkness is harmless." He turned and strolled out the mouth of the alley and onto another Chicago sidewalk.

Scattered snowflakes began to fall. Pete hunched his shoulders in an effort to stay warm. The wind snatched some of the falling snow, tumbling the flakes in a frenetic halo around the other man's wiry tendrils of hair.

"Armageddon is cancelled," the emaciated man announced. He held out his arms in a theatric pose. "I shall help bring about a fresh start."

"I thought the plan was to let humanity hurtle along toward the finish line." Pete said. They turned to face the biting wind and strode up the sidewalk. "Why delay the inevitable? And why drag me into it?"

"Because you need it; you can't drift aimlessly forever. You need purpose."

Skepticism spoiled Pete's features. "What's your scheme this time?"

"I intend to run for the office of President of the United States."

At first, Pete thought he'd misheard. "You're joking."

"Have you seen the news lately? Humanity teeters on the edge of the precipice leading to extinction. I will lead them away from that precipice."

"You can't launch a political career," Pete said. "That's not what you do." He realized as he said it how absurd his words sounded.

"Everyone has heard of me," his companion countered. "I'm the perfect man for the job."

"You're not even a man."

The scruffy man went on as if he hadn't heard. "I've even started practicing my first major speech. Want to hear it?"

Pete realized they'd crossed from Lincoln Park into Old Town. Something about his companion fuzzed the edges of his short-term memory.

"Well, do you?" The other man had ceased walking and had turned to face him, hands on hips.

Pete threw up his hands in a gesture of surrender. "Sure."

"My fellow Americans," the would-be President said. "Fear not the darkness, fear not the howl. Even mice know the howl presents no danger, unless the H is silent."

"It always has to be a riddle with you, doesn't it?" Pete said.

"You didn't let me finish. The next line is, 'only when the howl loses the H must the mouse prepare to face the owl.' Get it?"

"Sure, I get it." *He doesn't stand a chance,* Pete thought. People hated parables these days, and hated someone trying to teach them a lesson even more.

Pete glanced at his wristwatch and saw the hands spinning backward. He loosed the strap from the buckle and tossed the timepiece into the gutter. Pete glanced around, assessing the neighborhood. Old style pubs and trendy eateries lined the streets. Pedestrians hurried past them, heads down. Pete thought he might be able to slip away from his companion in a crowded, darkened club. "You want to catch a comedy show? Second City isn't far."

The other man's eyes twinkled. "Verily I say unto thee: I'd feel more comfortable over at St. Michael's Church."

"Thank you all for being here." The speaker flashed a broad, toothy smile.

Pete frowned and nudged his companion. "We're volunteering at a soup kitchen?"

"Hush. Just wait and watch." He turned his attention back to the speaker, a slender woman at the front of the group. She had wavy brown hair and a voice that carried to the corners of the church basement. Horn-rimmed hipster glasses magnified her animated blue eyes as she scanned the faces of those assembled.

"The compassion you show to the people we serve is an inspiration. We both know how difficult it can be for the people who find themselves in need of our services. Your words and actions go a long way toward helping them keep their dignity. So treat everyone with respect and kindness, no matter what the situation is." The woman caught Pete's gaze, held it for a brief moment, and moved on. "Every year our food lines are longer. It's only with the assistance of local volunteers such as yourself that we can rise to meet the challenge."

The woman's gaze landed on Pete's companion and stayed there. "Sir, we aren't serving yet. I need to ask you to return to the parking lot and join the others waiting at the gray door." She gave him a thin-lipped smile.

The woman turned and motioned for the small group to follow. "If the rest of you will follow me, we'll head to the kitchen." Her voice trailed away as Pete and his companion slipped from the group. They climbed a narrow stairwell and pushed the door open, emerging into the blustery afternoon air.

"How's it feel to be judged by the color of your skin?" Pete asked.

"I'm not surprised, but why did she give you a pass?"

"I'm dressed nice." Pete waited a beat, and then asked, "Still want to save this world?"

His companion shrugged. "I'm sure you and I can both agree humanity still has its bright spots."

"I think kindhearted, virtuous people are about as rare as albino crocodiles."

"Oddly specific," His companion gave him a sidelong glance. "And while that may be true up to a point, it doesn't mean—"

Pete held up a hand. He didn't want to hear a sermon. "I'm just saying maybe there aren't enough good people left to make it worth the effort."

A tear trickled down the gaunt-faced man's cheek. "If you're in, you have to be *all in*. You can't minister to lost souls only when you feel inspired to do so."

Pete shrugged and looked away. "Fine, we could go back downstairs and ladle out some soup, or you could expedite things and sort their souls. But don't blame me if none are deemed worthy."

The pair wandered instead. They stopped at a hot dog cart and indulged themselves in the jovial vendor's wares. They crossed a street where the strains of Chicago blues floated from the windows of a pub. Someone sang in a ragged, mournful voice: "... drops gleaming on lamp posts sway like bootleg drinkers in the fog."

At the next corner, perhaps inspired by the music's earthy, heartfelt sentiment, Pete's companion unleashed a sudden torrent of words.

"His head was caught up in the clouds, his heart filled up with the Lord. But while he gazed up at Heaven, white-skinned slavers wrapped his feet in chains. They led him to the coast; they led him to the sea. They shipped him 'cross the ocean, but they did not set him free."

Someone shouted, "Amen to that, brother!" Several of the other pedestrians waiting to cross the street applauded. One woman stepped in close for a hug, despite the speaker's unkempt appearance. Pete examined each of their faces in turn. They all seemed enthralled, regardless of race, age, or gender. His friend radiated an irrefutable charisma when it suited him. *Friend?* Pete realized he was letting down his guard. They strolled on, and for the next three blocks, Pete ruminated.

The dark-eyed man startled Pete from his reverie by shooting out his hand and grasping the arm of a brawny fellow in a rumpled suit who had crossed their path.

"Get your damned hands—" the man's threat went unfinished as he fell into a violent coughing fit. Pete's companion released the man, who staggered to the curb and fell to his knees, hacking. At last, the man wiped his mouth with the back of his hand, rose unsteadily to his feet, and hurried away, still coughing.

"Go see." The gray-bearded man invited, as if indulging a curious child.

Pete stepped to the curb. The brawny man had coughed up a bloody human thumb. "Mafia enforcer. He'll keep coughing up parts of his victims until he turns himself in to the authorities," his companion said. "I put the Fear in him."

This is a new wrinkle. Pete visualized the big man's approaching ordeal and repressed a shudder. "You're full of surprises today," he said, hoping he'd disguised his grudging admiration.

"If I'm going to forestall the Apocalypse, I'll need to get everyone's attention first. And I'm aware how numb and cynical people are, believe me."

The sun had descended toward the horizon. The pair found themselves outside a mom-and-pop fried chicken shack. People hurried in and out, grabbing an easy meal before heading home after work. Pete's companion turned to face him.

"It's time to get off the fence, Pete. If I run for President, will you be my campaign manager?"

"No," Pete shook his head. "I am neither interested, nor qualified."

"I know you make a comfortable living with the fishing fleet you own," the gray-bearded man countered. "How about making a hefty donation to my election campaign?"

"Sorry, but I'll pass."

The other man bit his lip, thinking. At last, he looked up, his eyes still clinging to remnants of hope. "Can I count on your vote, at least?"

"I'm not even regis——"

The shrill crow of a rooster drowned out his words. A portly woman shrieked and threw her fried chicken bucket several feet into the air. When it landed, a live rooster emerged, flapped its wings, and strutted away down the sidewalk. People scattered in all directions as it loosed another raucous cry.

Pete's companion gave him a mischievous grin and jabbed a bony elbow into his ribs. "Three times in a row you denied me! I'm not bitter, but some things never change, do they, Pete?"

Pete and his seedy looking companion bookended a park bench. Evening passers-by ignored the pair, who'd pulled themselves turtle-like into their overcoats. They sat in companionable silence.

Pete gazed into the night sky. It was all so vast it boggled his mind. *So what makes* this *tiny ball of water and mud so special?*

"Setting aside my own cynicism for the moment, I still find it strange that you've chosen Chicago, of all places, to embark——"

Pete never finished his sentence. A taxi jumped the curb and hurtled toward them. Both men leaped in opposite directions. The careening vehicle smashed the park bench to splinters and lurched to a stop. The door flew open and the driver emerged. Even in the encroaching darkness, the newcomer's bright, false smile illuminated his swarthy face. He recognized the man in an instant.

The olive-skinned cab driver bounded up to Pete's companion and enveloped the sunken-eyed man in a bear hug. "I've been driving all over the city, looking for you!" He pecked the man's cheeks and forehead.

"I bet you have," the gray-bearded man said. "But this time you are not welcome. You have no role to play."

Pete saw a black and white police cruiser crawling along the tree line at the far end of the park. *Local law enforcement. Men with weapons.* "Leave him alone!" Pete lunged and shoved the cab driver—a man who'd once been a friend and colleague—to the snow-dusted ground. He turned to his companion. "We need to go. Now."

The other man nodded. He looked down at the dazed cab driver. "Back to eternity with you, Iscariot." He pointed a finger like a child playing cops and robbers and mimed shooting. The cab driver imploded in a haze of dust and ash. Pete and his companion disappeared into the depths of the park as the police cruiser came to a stop behind the crashed taxi.

Trees towered on either side of Pete and fell away as he ran. His companion's unique charisma had finally rekindled something within him, something that made him *aspire* and *believe*. Pete felt euphoric, exultant. He picked up his pace and drew even with the one intent upon giving humanity a fresh start. His companion might be the only being in existence who could rebuild forgotten concepts like faith, hope, and love.

"The first thing you need is a shower and a haircut." Pete panted as they ran. "Then we'll sit down and brainstorm campaign slogans."

"You finally off the fence, Pete?"

"I'm all in. With you every step of the way, Lord." Simon Peter matched his redeemer's gliding strides, and the pair melted into the night, fearing not the darkness.

BOTTLED SPIRITS

CHAPTER 1

A PRISON OF PURITY

"DAMN IT!" SHERIFF SETH BULLOCK pounded a fist into his opposite palm. "Where the hell is that Indian?"

Truman Bonner turned his gaze down the darkened underground passage. The two men stood waiting in the earthen tunnel. "He'll be here."

"He damn well better be," Bullock growled. "Sister Mary isn't going to last much longer. If anything, the damp air down here has sped up her decline."

Truman squinted into the darkness.

"If this doesn't work, may God have mercy on us all," Bullock said.

"And if it does work?"

The sheriff seemed to consider, then looked Truman square in the eye. "May God have mercy on us either way."

"What happened to the miner who found it?"

Bullock frowned before answering. "I had to shoot him. He went after a fellow prospector with a pickaxe. Found that blob dripping from the dead feller's mouth. Thought it might be a slug. Not a bullet, but a slug like you find under a rock. I heard that some fellers will lick toads and go plum crazy. Thought it might be like that, but—"

"But this is something different." Truman finished.

"That's the understatement of the century," Bullock said.

A figure separated itself from the shadows of the tunnel.

"Finally!" Bullock fixed his gaze on the approaching Lakota medicine man. "She's fading fast. Do you have the damned thing?"

Makohloka gave a solemn nod and raised the object. Truman, standing between the men, shuddered. "We'd better get moving before it's too late."

Truman, Sheriff Bullock, and Makohloka entered the nun's freshly built cell. Lantern light barely pushed back the darkness.

"Sister?" Bullock said. "We're here like you asked."

Sister Mary Agnes Gwyn opened her eyes and struggled into a sitting position. Her breaths came in short, phlegm-rattling gasps. "Makohloka, do you have the talisman?"

The dark-skinned man nodded. Sister Mary coughed, and dark, wet flecks sprayed from her mouth.

Truman couldn't hold his tongue any longer. "Sister, you don't have to do this."

The nun raised one hand in a feeble gesture that indicated she would brook no further argument. Truman closed his mouth.

"Have you made your peace with your Savior, Sister?" Bullock asked. Truman thought he sounded embarrassed.

The nun nodded. "What happens next must be done. It is my choice. I ask only that you do it quick and follow the steps as we discussed."

The medicine man raised the arrow. The arrowhead resembled obsidian, but Truman knew the truth. This creature constrained in the shape of an arrowhead had quite possibly climbed from the depths of hell. Truman wished he had a Bible, though what good it would do, he couldn't say.

Sister Mary eased back onto the blanket spread on the hard floor. Bullock stepped back and placed his hand on the heavy cell door. Truman knew the plan. If this went wrong and the creature got loose, they would sacrifice themselves to protect others. Bullock would slam the door and lock the rest of them inside.

Truman glanced once more at the arrowhead. Mere hours before, he'd stood by when the old Chinaman, Shen Liu; the tall, bearded Preacher Smith; and the Lakota holy man, Makohloka, had clasped hands and earnestly prayed, each in their native tongue. They'd cast a powerful spell, yet the arrowhead had already begun to lose its shape as the defensive shield they'd created weakened. The plan, to be executed here in this cell, was to place the imp in a second, stronger prison before it escaped from the first. Sister Mary would serve as that prison.

Makohloka knelt and raised the arrow over his head with both hands. Sister Mary nodded and closed her eyes, arms at her sides.

He thrust the arrow down and slammed the tip through her ribs right above her heart. Her eyes flew open and blood spurted from her mouth. Makohloka bent and snapped the arrow's shaft, leaving the obsidian-like tip of corruption inside the nun's convulsing body.

"Time to go," Truman urged. The pair hurried out of the cell and Bullock followed, slamming the door behind them. He turned the key in the lock just as Sister Mary unleashed a scream so loud it overwhelmed Truman's eardrums. Tears spilled from his eyes. Bullock staggered and covered his ears with his hands. Makohloka, the color drained from his cheeks, mouthed an incantation Truman couldn't hear. Bullock pinched his bandanna to his nose, which had begun to trickle droplets of blood.

Truman slid the vision panel open for one last look. Sister Mary flew against the bars with brute force that shook dirt from the ceiling of her improvised cell. Blood and spittle sprayed from her mouth and her fingernails raked at her chest.

"You sheep-raping bastards," a voice croaked. "Let me out! It burns inside this pious bitch!"

CHAPTER 2

POSSESSED BY SPIRITS

T RUMAN LEFT ONE POSSESSED woman for another.

He rode his buckskin, Prior, from Deadwood to his home outside Sturgis after the caging of the perverse imp. He gazed through the spruce at the stars above and let his pony follow the trail. The night sky put Truman in a mood both inquisitive and introspective. Had the thing come from one of the stars twinkling in the night sky, or from somewhere deep in the bowels of the earth? Perhaps it had come from within, he mused. What if the imp was a physical manifestation of the dark potential within each member of the human race? He hoped their solution would prove to be a permanent one.

Prior chewed up the miles with long strides of his dark black legs. Truman had left Deadwood well after midnight. He approached the Bonner homestead nestled in the foothills west of Sturgis just before dawn.

A ghostly white face rose out of the darkness and Truman drew his Colt .45. Prior did not shy away from the sudden apparition, and after a moment, Truman saw why.

"Isaac!" he addressed his son. "Why are you awake at this hour? And why are you out here instead of inside, asleep?"

"Ma's been drinkin' again," the boy said. His brown hair stood up in a cowlick, and purple crescents hung under his eyes. "She got herself some sour mash from one of the neighbors, I think."

Truman felt a twinge in his heart. He believed a boy Isaac's age should have only the vaguest idea of liquor. He dismounted and handed the reins to his son.

"Get Prior unsaddled and stalled with plenty of fresh hay and water in his trough." He ruffled the boy's hair. "I'll go see about your mother."

Isaac led the horse to the barn. Truman headed toward the cabin. His boots crunched gravel with each purposeful stride. He pushed open the door. From inside the main room came the sound of ragged snoring. Helena Bonner—once Helena Flynn, still a feisty, opinionated young woman from the Emerald Isle—lay sprawled on the pine slats of the floor.

Truman knelt next to her and sighed. Helena had smarts that equaled any schoolmarm in the Dakota Territory, and impish good looks that rivaled any Deadwood dance hall girl. But when deep in drink, she transformed into something ugly and mean.

An empty mason jar lay on the floor beside her auburn curls. Another sat empty upon the rough-hewn table. A telltale wet stain covered part of the log cabin's wall, beneath which were the shattered remnants of a third jar. Truman pictured Isaac narrowly avoiding the thrown jar and his thoughts darkened.

He leaned over his wife and slapped her cheek. Helena snorted and turned her face away. Truman crawled and put one knee on the folds of her gingham skirt between her legs. He didn't want her to roll away until he'd had his say. Something cold and wet soaked through the fabric of his trousers where he'd knelt.

"Wake up, damn it." Truman gritted his teeth in self-righteous fury. He shook her until her eyes fluttered open, bloodshot and watery.

Helena mumbled something. Her eyes drifted closed and Truman slapped her other cheek.

"What do you want?" Helena sounded angry, as if he was the one staggering home at the break of dawn, drunk as a skunk and mean as a snake. After the things he'd seen and been a part of, this infuriated him more than anything else.

"If you're going to lie in your own filth," Truman growled, "then you can sleep in the barn like an animal."

Adrenaline infused his limbs with strength, and he hoisted his inebriated spouse over his shoulder. He stomped across the floor and out into the chilly gray dawn. Hints of pink colored the clouds in the east.

"Truman, put me down." Helena slapped his back.

"You went and got liquor again, after I forbade it!" An idea occurred to him. "Do you know where Isaac was when I got here?"

"In bed?" Helena didn't sound sure.

"He fell down the well, I rode in just in time to save him, no thanks to you and your drunken shenanigans."

"You liar."

They'd entered the barn and Truman found an empty stall. "And you're pathetic." He threw Helena into the bedding of straw and turned away.

"Stop treating me this way! I haven't done anything wrong."

"Sleep it off. Then we're going into Sturgis to see the Reverend. Maybe he can help you see the truth, since you won't hear it from me."

He left the barn and latched the door. Isaac stood in the yard, waiting. Concern etched lines into his face. Truman squeezed his son with a one-armed hug and guided him toward the cabin.

"She just needs to be taught a lesson. Things will get better after this, I promise."

But six hours later, when Truman reentered the barn to find Helena gone, he realized she'd made him a liar.

CHAPTER 3

DEALT A BAD HAND

TRUMAN FOUND HIMSELF NEAR the top of a mountain he didn't remember climbing. Confused, he looked behind him, hoping something might jar his memory. Nothing did. He turned and kept walking until he approached an area where the spruce and pine needles and other brush had been cleared away, exposing the dark earth. A sweat lodge constructed of tree branches and tanned buffalo hides sat in the center of the cleared area. The remains of a fire smoldered a few yards away, and Truman noted two stray stones—one larger, one smaller—still heating in the embers.

A Lakota man stepped out of the sweat lodge and raised his hand in a somber greeting. "*Hau, kola*," he said as Truman approached. "Hello, friend."

Truman responded in kind. "*Hau, kola*. I am Truman Bonner."

"*Micaje Napé Sica*. My name is Bad Hand."

"Are you alone, or are there others?"

"I am *esnella*—a loner. I come to *Paha Sapa* because my heart cries for a vision."

Truman nodded, feeling an immediate kinship with the other man. Though the colors of their skin differed, Truman noted that they shared the same eye color: the rich brown of a chestnut horse. "I seek a vision as well. My wife, Helena, left our home in Sturgis. We had... words. My son and I have been following her trail, but the trail has grown cold."

He looked around and realized Isaac was nowhere in sight.

Bad Hand gestured for Truman to enter the sweat lodge. The cowboy ambled forward.

"*Iyotaka*," Bad Hand said when they were inside, motioning Truman to sit. Heated stones from the fire pit outside filled a shallow pit in the center of the enclosure. Truman stripped off his shirt and waited for his eyes to adjust to the dark interior. Bad Hand positioned himself opposite, pouring water onto the stones. Steam billowed and Truman fought the feeling of claustrophobia that welled within him.

After several minutes, Bad Hand repeated the procedure with the water. He next removed a small clay pipe from a leather pouch and filled it with sacred tobacco. Bad Hand chanted a prayer and smoked. Truman waited, trying to keep his mind clear. He wiped droplets of sweat away from his brow, conscious of the deepening lines of worry taking root there. Finally, Bad Hand passed the pipe across the stones and sat back.

"We are on *ki wanagi tacaku*, the spirit path," Bad Hand announced.

Truman frowned. He raised the pipe to his lips with tremulous hands. He inhaled and his lungs felt scorched. Another inhalation and his lungs cooled. A sense of peace washed over him. He handed the pipe back. Bad Hand closed his eyes and began a chant.

Truman's ears hummed. He kept still and tried to relax, but felt as if he might melt in the heat. Even in darkness, shadows seemed to flit around the sweat lodge. The humming sound grew to an unbearable roar.

"*Paaaaa!*"

Then silence.

Truman looked not at a vision of his wife as he had hoped, but at his lanky son. Isaac hung from a tree, his hands lashed to a sturdy branch by unseen bonds. He realized his son had been shouting for him. "Find me, Pa, before it's too late!"

The cowboy blinked and found himself back in the sweat lodge. Bad Hand still chanted across from him. As Truman watched, the other man's eyelids fluttered and opened.

"I have seen both of our futures; one is grim, the other worse. A holy man will die tomorrow. I will pay the ultimate price. Soon my spirit will go to *Mahpiya*, to Paradise, but will not stay. It is good that we met here in the Spirit World."

Truman didn't know what to say, so he kept silent.

"I have done no wrong," Bad Hand said. "My heart is good, though I could have lived a better life. *Wakan Tanka*, the Great Spirit, has chosen for me a new quest. Go, Truman Bonner. First, you must find your son. Then I will join you on your greater journey. Find me again in Deadwood, at the Gem Saloon."

Bad Hand raised both arms, elbows out, thumbs under his chin. He lifted his head off his neck, hefted it like a small boulder, and tossed it into Truman's lap.

CHAPTER 4

LONG IN THE TOOTH

T RUMAN AWOKE WITH A STRANGLED CRY. He sat up and rubbed his eyes. His muscles protested and his joints felt stiff from sleeping rough. Bad Hand and the sweat lodge were gone. The entire landscape had changed.

"I just had the strangest dream…" Truman broke off and looked around. They'd made camp on the edge of a small meadow bordering on a thick stand of trees. Prior and Addie, Isaac's golden palomino, had been hobbled and munched grass contentedly. The sun had changed position. It had warmed his shoulders as they had eaten, but now it had begun to sink beneath the horizon. Glowing embers showed the remains of their campfire. Truman saw no sign of his son.

"Isaac!" Truman called. "If you can hear me, let me know!"

No response came. He'd given his son a Bowie knife on his last birthday and had taught him how to use it. But those skills wouldn't protect Isaac from an angry timber rattler or a fall amongst the granite outcroppings. Truman scrambled to his feet.

Truman chastised himself for dozing off. The boy had apparently given in to the temptation to explore.

Long shadows tied the trees together in a web of growing darkness as Truman followed his son's footprints through the forest. The narrow path snaked between tree trunks and disappeared in the distance.

Fighting to remain calm, Truman advanced and examined the underbrush for broken twigs, bent leaves, and other signs of recent passage. He saw prints and recognized the repairs he had done on Isaac's left boot heel. The rapid approach of a moonless night did not work in his favor. Though Truman considered himself a fair tracker, he could not see in the dark.

Truman soldiered on, calling his son's name. Dusk became night, and Truman's nerves wound ever tighter. The trees seemed to part before him, and close behind him as he passed. High above, Truman made out a few stars that had taken their places in the night sky.

He looked ahead and saw a figure materialize in the darkness ahead. Truman drew his Colt .45 Peacemaker.

"Ye need not fear me." The voice was that of an old woman.

Truman holstered his weapon and stepped forward, staying loose and wary.

The woman, tall and willowy, appeared to be alone. She wore a long, dark cloak of rough-hewn fabric, and her features hid in the shadows of a hood. She curtsied and asked, "Whither thou goest?"

The newcomer's antiquated choice of words slowed his understanding, but after a moment, Truman replied. "I am searching for my son. He wandered from our campsite. Have you seen a boy on the path? He just turned twelve, but already stands up to my chest. Curly brown hair, brown eyes, slender, talkative."

The woman appeared to shrug. "I saw a boy not long ago. Brown hair and eyes? Aye. Talkative? Nay."

"Where did you see him? Was he hurt?"

"Turn right at the fork in the path just ahead." She stretched out an arm and pointed. The sleeve of her cloak was so long that her hand never came into view.

Truman looked but could not discern any divergence in the path. After a moment's hesitation, he said, "Could you guide me? I need to find him soon."

As they traversed the dark woods, his thoughts seized upon his fiery Irish wife, the woman he loved, whose demons he so hated. A week ago, Helena had run off, or—if Truman were to be truthful with himself—he had run her off. Her drinking and his self-righteous anger had proved a disastrous mixture. Now his son had gone missing, too. Truman struggled against the panic that threatened to bust loose, a wild mustang escaping the confines of a corral.

The woman stepped nearer. "Some call me the Old Maid." Truman could not disagree. Based on her reedy voice and the webbing of deep wrinkles he could see around her eyes, she seemed to have reached an advanced age. "Long in the tooth" was the phrase Truman's long-dead father would have used. He also realized what accounted for at least part of his trouble understanding her. Green cloth wrapped the lower portion of her face.

Seeing him looking, the Old Maid tittered. It sounded like someone shaking a leather pouch filled with shards of broken glass. "It keeps away the chill. Now, come, let us commence our brief excursion."

She turned and led the way into the smokestack blackness. The path, such as it was, narrowed even further. Branches clutched and grabbed at Truman as he passed. He kept one hand on his hat brim so he wouldn't lose it.

Truman's mind turned to Isaac. His eyes never seemed to lose their hopeful gleam. Where feelings of guilt and loss drove Truman, Isaac simply looked forward to seeing his mother again.

"What will you say to her when we find her?" his son had asked as they'd gathered dry wood for the campfire.

The question had taken Truman off guard. He'd gazed at the trees surrounding them as if they might offer suggestions. "I'd ask her why she ran away." His own words had given him pause. Was he trying to fool his son, or himself? Truman had set his shoulders and plunged ahead on a course closer to the truth. "Then I'd ask her forgiveness for what I done. Tell her I was a damned fool. I'd ask her to come back."

"I'm going to tell Ma I love her," Isaac had said.

His son's words had touched Truman's heart. The boy's personality—a potent mix of innocence and wisdom—always surprised him and made him proud.

The gunshot crack of a dead branch startled Truman back to the present. The Old Maid whirled, lunged, and clawed at his face with the ferocity of a cornered mountain lion. Truman lurched and toppled over a fallen log. He spat dry, bitter pine needles from his mouth and rolled into a crouch.

His attacker threw the hood back and cast aside the cloak. What the starlight revealed appalled the cowboy. The woman's left arm was sinewy and muscular. Long nails grew like talons from that hand. Her other arm looked as if the flesh had been stripped from it, leaving only skin to mend itself around the bone. She had no right hand.

Her muscular legs, clad in deerskin leggings, looked as if they could carry her a hundred miles or more before tiring. As she came toward him, she tore the green cloth from her face. Truman stifled a cry.

The removal of the wrappings revealed a sagging jaw that hung like a broken stirrup from her face. Truman felt revolted at the sight of the sharp, wicked-looking teeth protruding from her mouth. He was sure his father had never met anyone quite so long in the tooth as this hag.

Knowing he faced immediate danger, Truman reached for his . 45, only to find his holster empty. She leaped upon him, used her stub to pin him to the ground, and raked at his face with her nails. This time the Old Maid's attack drew blood. Hot trickles blazed trails across his skin. Sweat immediately stung the wounds. He grunted in pain and felt the ground for his missing weapon.

The Old Maid unfurled a hideous length of tongue and lapped the rivulets of blood from his wounds. A carrion reek emanated from her maw as her tongue probed into the deepest of his facial lacerations. The pain made the treetops above him spin like the skirts of dancehall girls.

Truman's eyes found and fixed upon a silhouetted figure dangling from a tree branch about ten yards away. He knew at a glance that it was his son. Isaac's hands were tied together and fastened to a sturdy-looking branch. But why hadn't he called out for help?

Dread filled him, and he raked the earth with his hands, desperate to find his six-shooter. What his fingers found instead was a jagged rock. Truman seized the makeshift weapon and dashed it against the side of his attacker's skull.

Her resulting cry made Truman's ears ring, but he seized the opportunity to push her away. He half crawled, half scrambled along the forest floor. He heard the Old Maid skitter through the vegetation, close at his heels. Truman spun around a tree trunk back toward the hag. He twisted to let her talons slash past his face, and then sent two hard punches to her midsection.

The Old Maid only laughed.

Truman clasped his hands over his head and sent a crashing blow into her leering face. She staggered and sank to the ground.

Truman pressed his advantage and drove a knee into his adversary's nose. It collapsed with an audible crunch and her head jolted back. He cocked his leg for a kick, but faltered when she opened her jaws wide as if inviting this move. Teeth lined her gums like ivory knitting needles. The Old Maid whipped a leg out and took his knees out from under him. He tumbled to the ground and felt the air driven from his lungs. He also felt a solid object beneath his left forearm.

Truman fought to draw air into his deflated lungs as the Old Maid rose with an outraged cry. Truman grabbed the object and felt the bite of a blade deep in the flesh between his thumb and trigger finger. It wasn't his weapon after all. It was Isaac's Bowie knife.

Cool air seemed to drip into his lungs, like a slow trickle from a natural spring. The Old Maid had paused, as if cherishing the moment before plunging in for the kill. Feeling lightheaded, Truman transferred the knife to his uninjured right hand and slid so his back braced against the trunk of an aspen. The Old Maid lurched toward him. Blood trickling from the wound on her temple, and, from her flattened nostrils, added dark rivers to the already detailed parchment map of her weathered face. Her black eyes glittered atop a leering mouth that remained at the forefront of Truman's worries.

The attacker lunged through the air from six feet away and came down on him with a screech. He barely got the knife up in time, but her momentum assisted his cause, and the blade pierced her chest cleanly. He heard the wet crunch of her ribs snapping and realized that the entire left side of her chest had imploded from the force of the blade. His fist—still gripping the handle of the knife—disappeared, swallowed into the wound. Over her shoulder, Truman saw several inches of protruding steel. The blood slicked on the blade looked black in the starlight.

The Old Maid mewled and hacked up blood. It spattered onto his face as she convulsed atop him. Her eyes rolled back in their sockets, and at last, she grew still.

Concern for his son now returned to the forefront of his mind. He shoved his attacker away. Truman's fist made a wet, squelching sound as he pulled it from her chest; it reminded him of the first birth of a calf he had witnessed as a boy. Using an aspen trunk for support, he stood on shaky knees. He wiped his face with his dry sleeve. It came away sticky.

Truman staggered to his son. Isaac was alive, hung by his wrists from a low-hanging pine branch. The boy's unruly curls were no longer brown. Enduring untold trauma had greyed his hair. It looked like shortgrass lined with early morning frost. Arrows of guilt riddled Truman's heart. Father stood next to son in a sideways embrace. By stretching, Truman was able to use the bloody knife blade to saw through the strands the hag had used to keep Isaac captive. His son slipped from his grasp and dropped from the branch like a piece of overripe fruit.

Truman held out his good hand, and Isaac wordlessly took hold of it. Truman pulled the boy to his feet. He thought it would only be a matter of time before the boy unleashed a torrent of babbled words about the incident, but he realized he'd have to be patient. Isaac had obviously received quite a shock.

"Just rest easy, Son. You're safe now, and you don't have to talk about what happened until you're good and ready."

Isaac opened his mouth, but no words came. Instead, trickles of black liquid seeped from between his lips and down his chin. Isaac mimed taking a bite, chewing, and then swallowing. Truman gaped as Isaac pointed to where the hag lay and then back at his mouth.

Truman finally understood Isaac's silence, and an anguished groan escaped his lips. Isaac had looked death in the face and had lost a part of his physical self in the process. Despite the ordeal, a newfound strength seemed to be present in his son's eyes. Something familiar lingered there as well. Truman still saw a hopeful gleam in Isaac's gaze. The anticipation of reuniting with his mother still fueled the boy's love of life.

Awestruck and heartbroken in equal measure, Truman embraced his son and wept.

CHAPTER 5

MINER ENCOUNTER, MAJOR PROBLEM

It WAS AFTERNOON the next day by the time Truman and Isaac forded the stream in Spruce Gulch. They began the slow ascent of another wooded hill. The wind and trees conspired to play auditory tricks, and when they crested the hill, a startling cacophony of sounds greeted the pair. Prior tossed his head with apparent disapproval. "I know. We're back here far too soon," Truman muttered. Isaac gaped at the scene in the valley below them. The bustling cavalcade of activity at the bottom of the hill seemed to entrance him.

"Deadwood," Truman said, as if the name alone explained everything there was to explain. Isaac only nodded. They rode into town.

After the Old Maid's brutal attack, Truman had cast about in the brush until he located the cloth she had worn around her face. He had used it to bind his wounded hand, relishing the irony of his attacker's disguise becoming his tourniquet. Isaac had recovered the Colt .45 from the underbrush, and the pair had hobbled arm-in-arm back to their campsite and their horses. Truman thought it prudent to seek the services of the nearest doctor for Isaac's injury.

Men shouted, laughed, and called to one another. Grubby miners, cursing and spitting, led pack mules through the streets. Dusty cowhands tilted their heads to look up at the kept women who flirted from the windows of their rooms. Some of the men turned away while others shuffled toward the brothel doors, looking both excited and foolish. Chinese men showed obsequious smiles as they pulled their carts, disappearing like ants into dark passageways. The tinkle of a piano came from one saloon. The batwing doors of another burst open, and a barkeep tossed a dapper-looking gambler who they must have caught cheating into the dust. One or two respectable women of society ventured along the streets, while legitimate businessmen and shadier characters smoked cigars and gave each other shrewd looks. A group of Lakota Sioux Indians, in town for the day to trade, made an eye-catching spectacle of buckskin and feathers.

Truman and Isaac found a painted sign indicating the office of someone named Dr. Twiley. They hitched their horses to a rail and ascended the stairs. The man in question turned out to be a dentist, but he said he'd been a surgeon serving the Union during the Civil War. Truman decided to trust the man's judgment.

"The tongue heals itself," Twiley said after inspecting Isaac's mouth. "Give it a week or two. In the meantime, a nip of rye now and then will help ease his pain."

Truman thought about telling the dentist he didn't approve of spirits, but he kept silent. Twiley gave Isaac's shoulder a squeeze. "And son, you'll likely have to relearn eating. Take it slow, so you don't choke."

After thanking the man—the dentist refused any payment—

Truman and Isaac descended the stairs and returned to the bustling street of the booming mining town.

"Excuse me," Truman said. "I'm looking for my wife." No one paid any heed. Truman raised his voice and repeated his plea. A few heads turned, but those folks lost interest after a moment and moved past them.

Truman walked to the center of the street and removed his .45 from his holster. He fired it in the air.

Heads turned. Some people froze while others scampered away. Truman looked around, dismayed to see at least half a dozen revolvers and shotguns drawn and aimed at him and his son.

"My wife is missing, and may be in grave danger!" he shouted. "This is our son. We're asking for help finding her."

Isaac gazed at his father. Truman drew strength from the boy's calm presence. No time to back down now.

"Her name is Helena," he called. "Curly red hair, freckles across the bridge of her nose. Pale skin—like milk. Green eyes—like duckweed."

"How'd a beauty like that end up stuck with a skinny sodbuster like you?" someone called. Several men laughed.

"If I found her, I'd keep her fer m'self!" This time Truman saw the speaker, a sunburned cowboy wearing wooly chaps despite the heat. Anger rose within him.

Truman felt someone touch his arm and started. He looked down to find a wizened old Chinese man beside him where no one had stood a moment earlier. He wore a black silk jacket embroidered with decorative white thread. His dark eyes seemed to flicker in the sunlight, and a long white mustache hung like cobwebs from both sides of his thin mouth. "I am Shen Liu. I helped you then, I help you now."

Truman finally recognized him. "Yes, of course! You helped us create the special arrowhead."

The old man bowed.

"You've seen my wife?"

The old man shook his head. "No, but for information, follow me, please."

Truman and Isaac exchanged a glance. "What about my son?"

"He comes, too."

The pair followed Shen Liu's diminutive frame until Truman saw wooden steps descending along the side of a building. Looking down, he had a momentary flashback to the events involving Sister Mary Agnes Gwyn. He thought he saw her ghostly white face floating in the darkness below, but he blinked and the apparition disappeared.

They descended the steps, and Shen Liu pushed open a red-painted wooden door. The trio stepped into a dark stone passageway lit by lanterns that hung from nails in the walls every twenty yards or so. Truman shuffled along the chilly passage, keeping Isaac close. Ahead of them, the rumble of a wooden laundry cart grew and then faded away until Truman heard only their footsteps on the packed earth and the gentle hiss of the oil lamps.

Shen Liu led them down a different passage, one so small Truman had to stoop to enter, though Isaac followed with ease. They trailed the old man down the pitch-black tunnel. Their guide told them when to turn left or right, or when to step up or down. After a period of prolonged travel, Truman began to feel claustrophobic.

"Where are you taking us?" he muttered. "I'm a cowpuncher searching for my wife, not a miner searching for the mother lode."

A hand grabbed the back of Truman's collar and hauled him backward into a dimly lit den. He spun around and reached for his .45, but he was shocked to find his holster empty. On the verge of panic, Truman realized Shen Liu stood in front of him brandishing his gun.

"You are slow," the Chinese man said. He handed back the gun. Truman took it, stupefied. Behind him, Isaac peered into the room. The old man gestured toward a luxuriant rug. "You lose your wife, but are not a miner. A miner knows about your wife, but he is lost, himself. Very strange. You help each other. Sit, please."

Shen Liu eased himself to the floor and sat cross-legged before a wooden tray decorated with ivory inlays and opalescent seashells. Atop the tray sat a variety of items: two smaller metal trays, a tiny oil lamp, and a pipe with a bamboo stem and a blue and white porcelain bowl. Isaac sat down across from the old man.

Alarmed, Truman stooped and pulled Isaac back to his feet. "An opium den is no place for a boy."

Shen Liu said nothing. He trimmed the wick on the little oil lamp and filled a pipe using something that looked to Truman like a skeleton key with a tiny spoon at one end. Shen Liu raised his pipe to his lips and inhaled. After a moment, he closed his eyes, and his shoulders sank as he relaxed.

"We build tunnels for laundry business, but have secret places." The old man arched an eyebrow at Truman as smoke swirled within the dim alcove.

Truman thought again of Sister Mary's cell, and nodded.

"A terrible crime happened in Deadwood, then another. Evil men flee. Where they go, I do not know. Only luck that I hear you in the street, asking."

Truman shifted his weight from one foot to the other. "How does the miner figure into all this?"

"This miner, a newcomer named Clarence Conroy, found a letter as he reached the Black Hills. Someone put pages under a rock. At first, the fool thought he found a map to hidden gold. He came into my emporium. I heard him complaining about his bad luck."

Shen Liu had closed his eyes, lost in reverie.

"I own the Dragon Emporium. My wife and I sell food, spices, and medicines imported from China. They are true luxuries. The miner read the pages aloud. The writer reveals the outlaws' names. This Conroy decided he wanted reward for the pages. We send for Sheriff, but he did not come right away. My wife prepared delicious soup for miner. He eats, loses himself. You help him, and then he helps you."

Truman frowned. "I don't follow that last part."

Shen Liu held the pipe over the flame, and then returned it to his lips. "The first terrible crime happened here in Chinatown. My wife tried to help. Miner got the wrong soup."

Father and son exchanged glances. Isaac shrugged. Truman felt like shrugging in response. Instead, he asked, "How is my wife involved?"

Shen Liu retired to a corner of the tiny room. He twirled one end of his wispy mustache with a long-nailed finger.

"At the bottom of the pages is name: Helena Flynn Bonner."

Truman's pulse raced. Had Helena fallen in with a band of outlaws? Or had she been taken by force? His guts rolled like a snake uncoiling from its den. He swallowed hard, the dry click sounding in the crypt-like silence of the room.

"How can I help?"

"The cell," Shen Liu said. "You must take the miner to the cell inhabited by the *yāomó*, the demon."

Truman shuddered at the prospect. Cold sweat broke out across his forehead. He wiped his face with a bandana. "Why don't you do it?"

"I have much to lose. You have much to gain."

Truman felt the blood drain from his face. He leveled his gaze at the old man for nearly a minute.

"Where is the miner now?" Truman asked at last.

CHAPTER 6

GHOST SOUP

TRUMAN BONNER GRUNTED from the effort as he backed down one of the Chinese laundry tunnels beneath Deadwood. His son, Isaac, followed. Between them, hogtied and drenched in sour sweat, writhed the lunatic prospector, Clarence Conroy. Their soup-eating captive would have been howling in protest if not for Truman's bandana wadded up in his mouth. The flickering oil lanterns nailed to support beams cast just enough light to assure them they hadn't gone blind.

As they moved along, Truman wrestled with guilt over involving his son in such a ghastly endeavor. He had to admit that Isaac had been through worse and showed more bravery and presence of mind than most men show three times his age. In truth, there was no one Truman trusted more in a situation like this.

"We should have asked Shen Liu to let us use a laundry cart," Truman remarked. Isaac grinned.

Truman recognized the cryptic sigils that Liu and his compatriots had inscribed on the walls. They drew near the spot where Sister Mary Agnes Gwyn remained covertly cloistered. Her papal enclosure was only a crude cell, its grillwork made of heavy iron bars, all of it shrouded in perpetual darkness.

Truman and Sheriff Bullock had arranged with certain members of the Chinese immigrant community to facilitate the building of this secret prison. And all because of a perverse imp that someone, in their quest for gold, had discovered deep in the bowels of the Earth.

Still carrying Clarence, Truman and Isaac shambled along until they reached a dead end. Truman pressed one of the stones, and part of the wall receded. The cowboy lit an oil lantern he found hanging from a spike just inside the newly revealed entrance and held it aloft. He looped the fingers of his free hand under the length of rope binding the prospector's wrists and lifted. The rope bit at Truman's palm, but he ignored the pain.

They made their way through the passage until they reached the heavy, locked door that led to the antechamber of the nun's cell. Panting, they dropped Clarence onto the dank floor, and Truman fed the key Shen Liu had given him into the lock. The door creaked open, and Truman approached the iron bars, lantern in hand. Behind him, he heard shuffling boots as Isaac dragged the prospector into the chamber.

"Who have we here?" The voice that came from behind the bars sent a bitter chill racing down Truman's spine, like a January wind howling across the Dakota Territory prairie.

"This is Clarence Conroy."

"Bring him to me."

Truman hesitated. "Not yet. Someone believes you may possess the power to heal this man. He's having violent tantrums. He chased after townsfolk with a pickaxe."

The figure, shrouded in a long black tunic, stood statue-like behind the bars. A black veil covered not only the nun's hair but hid her face as well. "Your mouth is filled with lies born out of selfish concerns. I will not be lied to."

The nun turned away and made as if to lie back down in the corner of the cell.

Truman relented. "He's secreted away a journal belonging to my wife. She's missing. The journal could help us locate her, but in his current state, he's unable to help us."

"Remove the cloth from his mouth and bring him to me," the voice repeated.

Truman made brief eye contact with Isaac, and then the pair lifted the crazed man to his feet. Truman removed the makeshift gag and the skinny prospector immediately unleashed an angry torrent of words. Truman thought he recognized the words as Chinese. Clarence fixed a wide-eyed gaze on Sister Mary and fell silent.

"Ask me what ails him," directed the voice from the cell.

"What ails—?"

"I'm talking to the boy."

Truman felt his face flush. "He can't speak. No tongue."

"Sorry to hear that. Truly, I am." The nun leaned toward Isaac as if waiting for a response. When he didn't react, the nun's head swiveled back to Truman. "Is he deaf as well?"

"No. He just has a low tolerance for bullshit."

The figure behind the bars surged forward. "Tell me how it happened! I love a good story!"

"Stop wasting time!" Truman said. "We're here to help Clarence. Do you know what ails him or not?"

"Of course. This fool has ingested a bowl of ghost soup."

"Ghost soup?"

"Chinese folklore among certain remote villages contends that digging up and boiling the bones of the dead will yield a soup of highly medicinal properties. It doesn't."

"What *does* it do?" Truman asked.

"Opens a portal for angry spirits to return to this realm. Hui ta Wong is here with us. He's wearing the body of Clarence like a shabby old suit. His confusion is strong, but his anger and hatred are stronger. He tells me outlaws—white outlaws—raped his wife, and then murdered them both for sport."

Truman glanced at the grizzled prospector as the voice continued.

"He'd like nothing more than to kill every white man he sees if given the chance. Shen Liu's wife made the soup. He served it to Clarence here by mistake. And he duped you into serving as his errand boy."

Truman ignored the jibe. "Can you remove the spirit? Take Wong out of Clarence and send his soul back where it belongs?"

"I can and I will. Bring him to me."

Truman didn't move. "Tell me what you intend to do first."

"We will share a kiss."

Truman felt his mouth fall open. "A kiss? Why?"

"I will pull the unwelcome spirit from him and save his life. The errant soul will have no choice but to return to where it came from. Then all will be as it should."

Truman looked at Clarence. "Does the dead Chinaman inside Clarence know we're talking about sending him back?"

"Would he be standing here like a docile lamb if he knew?" The figure in the cell uttered a few Chinese words, and the grubby little miner grinned.

"What did you say to him?" Truman asked.

"I offered to help him turn you inside out and dance on your steaming entrails if he kissed me through the bars."

Truman instinctively reached for his Colt .45.

"Oh, unclench," chided the voice behind the bars. "Would you rather fight him every inch of the way?"

Truman caught Isaac's eye and they each took one of Clarence's arms and guided him to the bars of the cell.

The nun lifted her veil, revealing papery, desiccated skin. Her rapid mummification shocked Truman. It reminded him of the dried outer layer of a yellow onion, and his stomach clenched as the odor of dead, dried flesh reached his nostrils. Truman found himself lamenting how death and the presence of the imp had corrupted Sister Mary's visage.

Hui ta Wong must have sensed the trap because he howled with terror and began writhing, trying to get away. Truman and Isaac braced themselves and held the smaller man against the iron.

Mary Agnes's skeletal face thrust between the bars and pressed against the raving man's lips. What looked to Truman like smoky gray syrup passed from the prospector's mouth and into the nun's. Truman felt the hair on the nape of his neck stand on end, as if it were trying to uproot and relocate to safer climes.

The miner convulsed. His eyes rolled up in their sockets. The bulging whites contrasted with the hollow pockets of darkness in the nun's skull.

Then Sister Mary fell to her knees and reached through the bars. It took a moment for Truman to realize the emaciated fingers had torn open the front of the prospector's wool trousers. Before any of them could react, the nun had taken Clarence's member in her mouth. Truman realized Isaac had loosened his hold on the old prospector's arm. He watched the proceedings with what looked like a mixture of curiosity and dismay.

Truman, feeling uncomfortable, turned his gaze to Clarence. The grizzled prospector had stopped struggling. If anything, it looked as if he'd pressed himself harder against the bars. The skeletal head bobbed, the nun's habit obscuring most of the motion. Truman felt his tenuous control of the situation rapidly dwindling. "That's enough!"

The nun paused and pulled away just enough to favor Truman with a yellow-toothed leer. "Hui ta Wong's soul proves to be rather stubborn. It doesn't want to leave. Do you want me to coax it out or don't you?"

Truman looked away. The possessed nun resumed her ministrations. Truman moved to Isaac and led him to the corner of the antechamber. "I don't know how this will play out, but I'm sorry you had to see this."

Behind them, Clarence emitted a squeal of pain. Truman spun around.

"Teeeef!" Clarence cried. "She's scrapin' me wif her teef!" Truman realized he could understand the miner again. That meant the Chinaman's soul had departed. He took a quick step forward and drew his sidearm.

Clarence had braced his grubby palms against the bars in an effort to pull away. Dark rivulets of the prospector's blood dribbled down Sister Mary's bony chin. Truman realized that she did not intend to release her captive unless he intervened.

"Let him go!" Truman thrust the barrel of the .45 through the bars and against the nun's skull. "Last chance!"

Sister Mary ignored him. Truman pulled the trigger. The thunder crack report reverberated from the walls and deafened them. Dry bone fragments blasted against the cell wall.

The nun fell away, and the prospector sagged to the ground. Truman crouched and glanced at the prospector's member. There was some blood, but the wound appeared to be superficial. Truman looked up at Clarence's slack face and closed eyes. "Is he dead?"

"He's cleansed," the figure in the cell snarled. It seemed to come from far away. Truman realized his ears still rang from the gunshot.

Truman held a hand beneath the limp man's nostrils. He felt the warmth of Clarence's ragged breathing and looked at Isaac. "Drag him out into the air, quick. Take him to a horse trough and splash water on his face."

Isaac cocked one eyebrow.

"Go ahead. I'll deal with her," Truman said.

The boy dragged the unconscious man along the stone floor. After they'd disappeared around the corner, Truman turned back to the figure in the cell.

"The Chinaman's soul, were you able to retrieve it?"

"Oh my, yes. The moment I kissed him."

Truman felt his cheeks grow hot. "But you said—"

"I lied. I just wanted to have some fun."

Rage welled up in Truman, but his fury had nowhere to go. "Put the veil back down, for god's sake," he finally muttered.

"I do nothing for god's sake."

"Cover up, I said!"

"Does her face gall you that much?"

"It's you who galls me."

"How hurtful you are!" The nun yanked off her veil, then wrestled the habit up over her skull. The fabric rustled as it landed in the corner of the cell.

All that remained of Mary Agnes Gwyn now lay exposed. Truman winced. It wasn't her bleached white skeleton that galled him. It was the small, sinewy figure imprisoned in the dead nun's ribcage. The unholy creature, covered in reptilian scales and black as a mineshaft at midnight, leered at him with glittering gold eyes.

"What an ugly little cuss you are," Truman said. "And you've changed."

The imp preened. "I'm stronger now."

"What are you getting at?" Truman asked. Fingertips of dread caressed his spine. "What did you do with the soul?"

"I devoured it. Another ignorant mistake on your part and I'll have enough power to break free."

"I'll never let that happen," Truman growled. Righteous assurance rose within him like a roaring prairie fire. "Despite what happened here, despite what you just did, Sister Mary was innocent and pure. She made the ultimate sacrifice, letting you try to possess her body as she died. But the trap was sprung. Her soul is at rest now, and her mortal coil still serves as an effective prison for you!"

The imp gave Truman a sly look. Its talons made an abrasive sound as they scraped against the inside of her rib cage. The desire to return to Isaac came over the cowboy, sudden and strong.

"Her corpse is a cage, nothing more. And soon the cage will be empty," the imp said. The skeletal nun began a hideous, awkward dance, like a marionette pulled by invisible strings. From his ribcage prison, the black being gave Truman a jaunty little wave. "I'll see you again soon, and it won't be here. You can bet your life on it."

Truman grabbed the lantern and spun on his boot heel. He wanted to run, but forced himself to walk. He would not give the little demon the satisfaction. The imp's laughter assaulted Truman's ears as he slammed the door and turned the key in the lock, leaving the creature in absolute darkness. He hurried through the winding passages, up the steps, and out into the cool embrace of the night.

The ringing in Truman's ears from the gunshot went away the next day. The echoes of the imp's laughter seemed to linger much longer.

CHAPTER 7

DUST DEVILS

"I'M MIGHTY OBLIGED," Clarence Conroy said the next morning. "It was like bein' trapped in my own head. I could see everything but couldn't move, couldn't do nothin' to help myself."

Truman had paid for a room above the Saloon No. 10 for the three of them. Conroy took a blanket and had slept like the dead on the room's floor. Truman and Isaac shared the straw-filled mattress. Though Isaac slept, Truman spent most of the night chasing his own thoughts—and being chased by them.

Conroy stretched, making his joints creak and pop. Isaac sat on the bed looking from one man to the other.

"I'm glad we could help," Truman said. "Listen, Clarence, before you fell ill…"

Conroy nodded. "The journal I found. Yes."

"Will you take us to it?"

"No."

Truman balled his hands into fists, and then winced as the palm still healing from the Old Maid's attack flared. "We helped save you!"

The old man raised both hands in a gesture of surrender. "What I mean is I don't need to take you to the journal pages. I have them right here."

Thunderstruck, Truman could only shake his head.

Conroy sat on the edge of the bed, dipped two grimy fingers into his left boot, and withdrew several curled pages.

Truman moved the water basin from the top of the dresser to the floor. Then he took the pages from Conroy's outstretched hand and flattened them out on the dresser. His eyes caught sight of last week's date and his heart clenched with dread. Truman devoured the words on the pages with mounting horror.

August 14, 1889

Dear Journal,

I make these notes in an effort to stay sane. We've been traveling north across a vast expanse of sparsely growing grassland for what feels like days. Hunger pains cramp my stomach. Worse, no one has any liquor left. Mounting fears and frustrations have tempers flaring.

Dale Hollister is the leader of our group. I met him in Deadwood after Truman's holier-than-thou tantrum. I'd ridden Spirit from the homestead and wound up at the Gem Saloon. We shared a few drinks. Then he invited me to accompany him on a "scenic ride out of the Hills." I felt restless enough to say yes.

Two other acquaintances of his, Joseph Cagle and a young man named Jamie McCrossen, have joined us. I get the impression that these three share a dark history. I overheard Cagle talking with Hollister. The trio felt it necessary to leave

Deadwood due to an unfortunate incident with a Chinese laundryman and his wife. I heard Hollister say, "I don't think anybody who matters will give a damn, but if it will help you rest easy, we'll light a shuck north for a while." I do not know what incident they refer to, but I fear I have fallen in with the wrong type of men. I stay close to Hollister. He had—until recently—some fine whiskey on his person, and he's kept me safe from the others, if you take my meaning.

I suppose they are outlaws. There, I said it. Might as well be honest with myself.

Why I left my family behind in Sturgis, I'm not sure I can say. I know I wish to return home, but circumstances have created a situation where I feel I cannot. Truman is a good man, but life with him bores me! It's as if he's always trying to protect me. From what, I do not know. His disapproving frown follows everything I do. Isaac is a good boy, and the memory of his face pains me awfully, but I don't doubt he can get along without me. He's close to becoming a man anyway. They are better off without me.

Hollister leads our procession. He is followed by McCrossen, and then I follow, as I try to scratch these words, allowing Spirit to move at his own pace. The corpulent Cagle brings up the rear, lagging behind us. I think his poor mount may have lost a shoe.

Later: As the temperature increases, the men become more quarrelsome.

I just overheard McCrossen talking to Hollister. This time over some awful business about a dead preacher. Hollister and McCrossen each blamed the other for the holy man's death. But then Hollister laughed and congratulated himself on running down an Indian to take the blame. I thought they'd left town because they'd robbed a Chinese couple.

I should not be here. Must be vigilant and careful.

Later: I don't know how long Cagle has been gone. The sun is still high, but water is low. The horses are close to being played out. We rode with our heads down in a useless attempt at ducking the sweltering heat. I looked back to check Cagle's progress, but the large man was nowhere to be found.

I called out to the others, and we made a brief attempt at retracing our path. We found his hat but nothing else and gave up the search. This may sound heartless, but the lack of water played fearfully on our minds. According to Hollister, if we wanted any chance at finding water, we had to keep moving. So we press on.

The sun hangs high in the sky. Due to some trick of the light, it looks as if it hasn't moved. Hollister has assured McCrossen and me that a sinkhole must have brought about our companion's demise. Hollister rode alongside me for a time, trying to raise my spirits. I found myself wishing he had spirits of another sort to offer. I find that my irritation and discomfort grows with each minute. I suffer the ill effects of prolonged exposure to the sun as well. My skin burns, my ears ring, my head aches. I no longer feel the hunger pains, but the desire for a drink is unbearable.

The mirages are the worst. The naked trunks of large, limbless trees appear to ripple and cavort in the distance in all directions. As I watch, they disappear like salmon leaping upriver to spawn.

Later: Hollister is gone. He rode away hard and fast back the way we'd come. I don't know whether to think of him as a coward or applaud his good sense.

McCrossen drew his six-shooter and shouted for Hollister to stop, but to no avail. Then he turned his weapon on me and accused me of leading them toward a sheriff's posse. I told him I'd done nothing of the sort and pointed out that Hollister had been leading us. We reversed direction. McCrossen made me ride ahead of him, following Hollister back in the direction of Deadwood. He said if a posse waited in ambush ahead, then Hollister had the right idea by going back. I didn't know what to say to that logic. McCrossen also said if we ran into any trouble, he'd gun me down without hesitation.

Later: I write this after the fact. Here is what happened:

McCrossen still groused behind me as we continued our journey.

I had my head down, to hide my face from the sun, so I saw it happen: a hole in the earth opened on the path in front of me. Spirit reared back on his hind legs and threw me into the dust. Something emerged from the hole and snatched my horse away.

It looked like a gigantic, eyeless snake with a cavernous mouth.

McCrossen pulled me onto his horse and urged it into a gallop in hopes of leaving this cursed stretch of land behind us, but the horse soon slowed, too played out to run any farther. It felt as if we moved at a snail's pace.

I realized then that the mirages were not mirages at all.

They look like dust devils tearing at the sand, but rather than disappearing into the sky, they sink back into the ground. Like when termites overrun a dead log, something unholy infests this stretch of deserted land.

I need a drink so badly.

Water would do, but it's not my first choice.

Later: McCrossen threw me off his horse. I landed hard but managed to avoid serious injury. Perhaps I'm getting used to falling.

I know that I am in great danger. McCrossen rides ahead muttering to himself. He has revealed the awful truth about the Chinese laundry couple. All three played a part in that horror. According to McCrossen, it was Hollister's idea to kill the preacher, too. He keeps waving his pistol around and looking back at me in a way that scares me. I think he called me the Angel of Death. Or perhaps he sees it lurking behind me. He could leave me behind, yet he does not. Is he too terrified to test his own theory? Maybe he feels as if he deserves this hell. Perhaps we both do.

I scratch these words to pass the time and keep my mind from unraveling.

I believe one of the dust devils will come for one of us at any moment. They dive, you see. They swim through the sand, and then open up the ground beneath their prey.

McCrossen doesn't realize all this yet, but I do, and perhaps I can use this to my advantage. He rides ahead on his horse. I believe he's put himself at a deadly disadvantage.

Weight may be the key to my survival. Tread lightly, Helena.

There is some good news: I believe the temperature may have dropped a degree or two. Even better, I see in the distance a most welcome sight: the Black Hills. We're close to home!

Later: McCrossen tried to abandon me. He sank his spurs into his horse's flanks, hoping to leave me to my fate.

Instead, the sand became a whirling vortex beneath him. McCrossen and his terrified pony were sucked down and *away. I was alone.*

Trembling, I sat down to inscribe this final entry. I remain as still as possible. The sun sinks low now, and this hellish day will soon come to an end. The safety of the boulder-strewn foothills is close.

I am, as my overprotective Truman often commented, a "little slip of a thing." I believe I can make it over the last bit of desert without attracting attention from the dust devils, whatever they truly are. Then, perhaps, I can go about finding a town, and in that town, a saloon.

I have a good feeling about my chances. It's nothing I can present facts to support, it's just a feeling. Call it a woman's intuition.

In haste, as the last of daylight dims,
Helena Flynn Bonner

CHAPTER 8

BOON IN A BOOMTOWN

"THAT SUMBITCH THERE kilt Preacher Smith!"

The pear-shaped bartender at the Gem Saloon in Deadwood pointed with his double chin toward the far end of the bar. The scent of fresh sawdust mixed with the sour tang of vomit and the cloying perfume of the soiled doves who worked in the bedrooms upstairs. Truman Bonner turned to look in the direction indicated by the speaker.

"Dirty Injun kilt the most God-fearin' man in town." The bartender scowled his disapproval. "But vengeance is mine sayeth the Lord, or at least sayeth my boss, Mister Swearingen. He put a bounty on the head of Preacher Smith's murderer. A posse brought that in to prove they got him. Found him skulking around the edge of town where Preacher Smith died. Drinks were on the house for those fellers. Say what you want about Al Swearingen; the man sure knows how to get a head!" The barkeep slapped a filthy towel on the wooden bar and brayed laughter.

Truman said nothing. He paid the man for a bottle of rye for Isaac's medicinal use and strolled to the far end of the bar for a look. The bartender had not indicated a man, but a large glass jar. It was a one-gallon size, perhaps once holding milk, pickles, or boiled eggs. Now a human head, brown and misshapen, was its only content. Coarse black hair floated like tendrils in the fluid surrounding it.

"He ought to be happy," the bartender called. "He's pickled in ninety proof!" A few grizzled miners laughed, and Truman forced a wan smile. He reached out and turned the jar with his fingertips. The decapitated head's features came into view.

The eyelids popped open and Truman jolted in shock—and in recognition.

Truman Bonner, I am glad you are here. Take me away from these fools.

"Bad..." The stunned cowboy started to speak aloud but stopped. *Bad Hand?*

Yes.

The lips did not move, but Truman felt as if he heard every word in his own native tongue. He sent a thought back. *How is this possible?*

This is your spirit path, and mine. Our paths have converged.

Truman glanced around the bar. The few other patrons paid no attention to him, and the barkeep had busied himself with the task of smearing his filthy towel inside each of the saloon's shot glasses. Truman found himself wondering if all of this was another dream. After all, he'd never encountered Bad Hand in real life.

As if in response, the head in the jar locked eyes with him. *We met before in the spirit realm. You seek your beloved, Helena. She is with the men who murdered me. This much I know.*

Truman felt strange, as if his blood had become an icy slush that his heart struggled mightily to keep moving. *Where are they?*

Northwest of this place. Take me with you and we may help each other.

Truman closed his eyes. Was he going mad? Suffering a breakdown brought on by the stress of Helena's desertion? Perhaps. And yet, after all he'd seen and been a party to in the past few weeks, Truman didn't feel inclined to dismiss anything without careful consideration.

Shen Liu had led him to Clarence Conroy, the miner who found Helena's journal pages. She described unbelievable horrors, but the details about their location seemed to match what Bad Hand had just revealed.

He reopened his eyes and looked again at Bad Hand. The

Lakota's eyes were now closed. Seeing the bartender engaged in garrulous conversation with a pair of just-arrived ranch hands, Truman reached out and lifted the heavy jar, stowing it in the crook of one arm. Then he grabbed the bottle of rye with his bandaged hand. He turned and hurried through the saloon. To his own ears, his boots pounded the wooden slats like galloping hooves. The beckoning sky outside the batwing doors seemed to shrink to a pinpoint, too far to ever be reached. Truman mentally prayed to escape the barkeep's notice.

"Hey! Come back with that!"

Truman broke into a run and burst through the Gem Saloon's entrance. His eyes found Isaac waiting with the horses. The boy saw him and immediately unwound both sets of reins from the hitching post. As Truman ran, Isaac put a booted foot in the stirrup and swung his leg over Addie. Truman jumped from the boardwalk and held out the bottle of rye.

"Just gargle and spit," Truman instructed as Isaac took it. He vowed to caution his son about the evils of alcohol later. Right now, they had to ride away before the angry barkeep caught up to them. Truman switched the jar containing the head to his other arm, grabbed the saddle horn with his good hand and began to mount. An angry shout from behind him gave Truman all the incentive he needed to leap into the saddle. He gathered Prior's reins in his good hand and turned in time to see twin black holes so close to his face they seemed to fill his entire field of vision.

"What in Sam Hell are you doin', cowboy?" the barman asked from the painless end of the shotgun. "That's the property of the Gem Saloon."

"Preacher Smith was a friend. And so was this man." Truman said these words not for the fat man's benefit, but for Isaac, who had lifted an inquisitive eyebrow at the jar's contents. "I don't believe he committed any crime. He's not a mongrel or a trophy, but a good and gentle man who deserves a proper burial."

"He's a murderer, and you're a thief," the barkeep said. Truman thought he meant to say more, but the fellow stopped short at the metallic click of a cocked hammer. Truman looked at Isaac. The boy's bone-white hair gleamed in the sunshine. His face remained emotionless. The barrel of Truman's Colt .45 rested against the barman's temple. Isaac had leaned over and taken it from Truman's holster while the two men spoke.

"You willing to lose your life for something that you consider a novelty piece?" Truman asked. "My son and I have been through some harsh trials lately. He got his tongue bit off by a crazed cannibal woman we encountered in the forest a few days ago. If you killed me, he wouldn't think twice about sending a bullet right through your brains. Then you and me could race to 'our Father who art in Heaven' and to try to explain to Him what just happened."

The bartender's cheeks took on an ashen hue. "Mebbe we all just count to three an' go about our business."

"Wise choice."

The barman eased the shotgun away from Truman's face, and Isaac responded in kind. The people of Deadwood—grubby miners with their pack mules, sunburned cowhands, even a few hardy pioneer women—ventured along the streets, doing their best to ignore the gun-brandishing pair.

"I'd clear out if I were you. Al Swearingen will be awful hot when he finds out someone took his prized specimen."

Truman didn't argue with good advice. He stowed the jar in his saddlebag, then he and Isaac turned their horses and rode north out of Deadwood. After they'd left the last of the mining camp tents at the edge of town behind them, Truman removed the jar and gazed at Bad Hand. *Are they close? Is my wife hurt?*

Though he received no response, Truman hoped he'd hear from his new trail companion soon. Helena could not be far. He could not let himself believe otherwise. But who was she with, and under what circumstances? These questions haunted him.

He stowed the jar again and took up Prior's reins. They rode silently as the sun lengthened the shadows around them.

After an hour, Truman glanced back at his son. Isaac rode easy in the saddle, his face impossible to read. Truman was struck again by how much his son's ordeal had changed him, not just physically, but in the way he now carried himself.

The sun slipped behind the mountain. Soon they'd reach the place Helena had described in her writings. What then? Truman clung to the reins, pondering. The air around them cooled, a harbinger of the coming darkness.

CHAPTER 9

BETRAYAL BEGETS BETRAYAL

HELENA LANGUISHED ON A BED in one of the rooms of the Franklin Hotel on the south edge of Deadwood. A potent mix of liquor and laudanum fogged her mind and weighted down her limbs. She gazed across the room at the window. Hollister had drawn the curtain not out of consideration for Helena's rest, but because he wanted to keep her away from prying eyes. She heard flies buzzing against the glass in a futile attempt at finding freedom. Helena knew they'd die there.

A bottle of rye sat balanced on her chest. She noticed a stray fly had found its way into the bottle. It floated in the amber liquid. Would a dead fly stop her from finishing the bottle? She doubted it.

Hollister had been waiting for her. She'd outlasted McCrossen and evaded the dust devils, only to get bushwhacked by the man who'd abandoned her. "I ain't decided what to do with you yet," he had said, leering.

He said he would have to kill her if she tried to escape. They rode his horse back to town, where he'd taken this room. He'd dosed her with the potent narcotic and encouraged her to drown her shame with drink. Satisfied that her spirit had been broken, he'd left her, turning the key in the lock from the outside to keep her confined, a fly in a bottle.

You could run the race, fight the good fight, but what was the point when the odds were stacked against you? She took another swallow. The fly disappeared.

Dale Hollister sat alone in Saloon No. 10, drinking and listening. At an adjacent table, a miner spoke with drunken enthusiasm.

"I saw a dungeon. A witch of enormous power is imprisoned there!"

"Shut up, Clarence, you're sloshed."

"It's true!" the first miner protested. "I seen her with my own eyes!"

Hollister tossed back the last of his drink and sidled over to the miner. "I believe you."

The older man glanced up in apparent surprise. "You do?"

Hollister leaned in and murmured. "Ten dollars in gold if you take me to her."

The miner stood up so quick he tipped his chair over with a clatter.

"We getting close yet, pardner?" Hollister had followed Clarence around the laundry tunnels for just about as long as he cared to endure. The miner had blundered around, hitting dead ends, doubling back, making whispered assurances.

"She's hid good, but I'll find her," Clarence said. "Don't worry."

"Oh, I never worry."

The pair rounded a corner and came face to face with a

diminutive old man with a long white mustache. He wore black silk and shook a long-nailed finger in admonishment.

"You two are louder than stampeding bison."

Clarence drew back in alarm. "You! I don't want any more soup. Never again!"

Hollister took advantage of the momentary distraction and drew one of his Colt M1894s. The old Chinaman turned to flee, but Hollister darted out a hand and caught his braid.

"Hold on, little fella. I need you to be my guide." He cocked the gun and placed the barrel against the back of the old man's head. "The nun. Take us to her."

The old man led the procession through the maze of tunnels. At an apparent dead end—Hollister thought they'd been here at least once before—the Chinaman pressed one of the stones and part of the wall receded. He lit an oil lantern hanging from a spike and held it aloft. They made their way through the passage until they reached a heavy door. Their captive slid a key into the lock and pushed the door open. He approached the iron bars, lantern in hand. Hollister followed, along with Clarence.

"Why, Shen Liu and Clarence Conroy!" said a voice from the shadows of the cell. "What a delightful surprise! And who's this tall drink of water?"

Hollister watched a figure garbed in a nun's attire rise out of the darkness.

"Who are you, lady?" he asked.

"Well, I'm certainly no lady!" the figure said, somehow sounding malicious and lascivious at the same time.

Hollister found himself becoming aroused. Dark power radiated from the prisoner. He felt it and he craved it. He kicked the door to the antechamber closed with one booted heel and used the barrel of his gun to direct the miner and Chinaman into the far corner.

"Let's talk," Hollister said. "I assume you want out of here. I might be able to help, but the question I have is: what's it worth to you?"

From within the cell, he heard what sounded like leathery wings unfurling; the nun was laughing. "You want something in return. What could that be, I wonder."

Hollister wet his lips. He was onto something big; he could feel it. "Power. I want a share of your power."

The nun nodded. "The bars imprison the nun. The nun imprisons me. I need strength. I need souls. I believe two will be sufficient."

Hollister eyed the pair standing in the corner. "These two?"

"Yes, bring my old friend Clarence over first."

Hollister grabbed him and dragged him to the bars. "You know this old coot?"

Again, the nun nodded. "He and I have been intimately involved." The miner blanched and made protests both outlaw and nun ignored.

"What now?" Hollister asked.

The nun drew back her veil and thrust her mummified cadaverous face through the bars. "Shoot him in the head!"

Hollister pulled the trigger. A deafening report filled the tiny room. Bits of bone, flesh, and brain sprayed against the near wall. Hollister watched the nun reach through the bars and grasp the old miner to keep him from falling. She sucked what looked like thick yellow smoke from the mouth of the dying man. Hollister ejaculated in his trousers.

The nun dropped the dead miner. "Now, the second."

Hollister turned, but the Chinaman had disappeared. He scanned the tiny room, thunderstruck. He'd stood between the old man and the door they'd entered the entire time. "How?"

"Doesn't matter," the nun said. "New plan." She reached for him through the bars and pulled him close. "How's your gag reflex, cowboy?'"

Five miles to the north, Truman and Isaac pondered the deserted expanse before them. They'd found no trace of Helena or the others she'd written about. No campfires or smoke on the horizon. The events detailed in the journal were dated several days prior. Were they too late? Dejected, Truman decided to camp for the night and return to Deadwood at dawn to inform Sheriff Bullock. Perhaps he could help them organize a posse or search party.

CHAPTER 10

BOTTLES GET EMPTIED

THE DAY HAD DRAGGED. Nightfall came, but Hollister never returned. Helena had emptied the bottle. She dozed in fitful bursts. Nightmares plagued her rest. Clouds obscured the moon. To Helena, the passage of time seemed interminable, a kind of purgatory.

At last, the sun began to rise. Helena did not. Pounding pain made her cover her head with the dirty sheet. Her brain felt too big for her skull. She ached, feeling battered and raw. And something, she reflected, was missing. Something integral. Helena frowned and chewed on her lip, trying to remember what she'd lost.

She dozed. Something happening in the street below woke her. *A disturbance of some sort*, she thought. She heard someone shouting. Then gunshots. A few at first, followed by a cacophony.

Helena slid from the bed and tottered to the window. She moved the curtain. Looking down upon the street, she saw carnage. Bodies lay strewn. She recognized the source of the violence: Hollister, a revolver in each hand, bellowing and shooting.

Then Helena saw what she had lost. She stepped away from the window and let the curtain drop.

Truman and Isaac returned to Deadwood dispirited and exhausted. Though the horses had rested and cropped grass contentedly, neither Truman nor Isaac could sleep. After a few hours, Truman had covered their campfire with dirt and the pair had saddled the horses. They'd returned to Deadwood with the sun and rode to the Sheriff's Office to await Bullock's arrival.

One of his deputies saw them waiting and stepped outside to greet them.

"Help you?" He spit a stream of tobacco juice into the dust.

"I'm Truman Bonner; this is my son, Isaac. I've helped Sheriff Bullock in the past. I need his help finding my wife. I believe she's been taken by force by some outlaws."

The deputy nodded and spat again. "There've been terrible goings-on here lately. Not the way the sheriff wants things to be in Deadwood. Folks are forgetting how to act civilized."

Truman, be on your guard! He's coming. The voice came to him urgent and clear. Truman excused himself from the deputy and returned to Prior. He opened his saddlebag and looked inside. Within his gallon jar, Bad Hand had reopened his eyes.

Who's coming? Truman sent the thought back as he pretended to rummage around in the saddlebag. *Bullock?*

He's coming, too; they all are. Bad Hand's features were emotionless, but his thoughts came at Truman so fast and strong that they felt like shouts. *Many spirit paths will intersect, as foretold in the vision we shared. The Great Spirit flies over us now, searching for souls.*

Isaac tugged on his father's arm. Truman looked up and saw Sheriff Bullock riding toward them from the south end of the street.

"Truman Bonner!" A cry came from the shadows across the street. Father and son turned to look. Shen Liu trotted across the road toward them. The sharp report of someone firing a gun pierced the morning air. The little man threw his arms up and tumbled to the dirt.

HE'S HERE! Bad Hand warned. *My killer! But he's changed somehow—*

Anything else he wanted to convey was lost in a hailstorm of lead.

Dale Hollister walked down the center of Main Street devoid of conscience, unfettered by fear. Something else had taken control. He fired matching Colt M1894s with preternatural skill and precision.

The deputy raised a Winchester rifle. Hollister pulled the trigger and took off the young lawman's hat. The top of his skull went with it.

Sheriff Bullock spurred his horse forward, drawing his gun. Hollister shot the horse out from under the approaching sheriff, sending him sprawling into the dust.

"Isaac, here!" Truman tossed his Colt .45 to the boy. Then he knelt and picked up the deputy's Winchester. He tucked the butt of the rifle against his shoulder and fired a hurried shot. Hollister didn't even flinch.

"Get behind the horses!" Truman urged. Isaac did as he was told, his features calm. Truman tried to emulate his son's demeanor, but it felt as if the world had gone insane.

Any early rising townsfolk had scattered. Bullock crawled in the dust. Truman saw that the sheriff had lost his weapon. Hollister closed in fast, still firing. Slugs kicked up geysers of dirt in the street, each one closer to the sheriff than the last.

"Shoot that man!" Truman shouted at Isaac. His son required no further urging or explanation. He began squeezing off shots at

Hollister. Truman chambered another round and did the same.

The big man turned his attention from Bullock to the Bonners. A tongue of flame belched from each barrel of Hollister's guns. One slug spun Truman around and drove him to his knees. Another tore through Prior's throat. Truman's horse toppled, its throat spurting gouts of blood.

Bullock continued to crawl toward his sidearm. Addie broke free and ran. Isaac knelt to reload, and father and son realized Hollister had them dead to rights.

Prior finished his fall and Bad Hand's jar rolled free. Truman scrambled for the Winchester but realized the ammunition he needed to reload sat inside the sheriff's office. He glanced down and saw a wet patch of crimson where the slug had grazed his shoulder. Isaac stood. Hollister stopped and faced him not ten yards away. Truman considered hurling his hat at the man, anything to draw fire, anything to save his son.

Isaac did not appear concerned. He seemed interested. The boy looked at something Truman couldn't see. He felt only astonishment as his son, facing the gun-wielding outlaw alone, broke into a grin.

Helena took a gulp from the bottle of 90 proof and tapped Hollister's shoulder. He turned, and she spat the whiskey in his face. Then she sloshed the rest of the bottle's contents over his shoulders and across his chest in a crude parody of a baptismal cross. He allowed her ministrations for only a moment before swatting her away with a slash of one scorching hot Colt barrel, then turned to face his other adversaries.

Hollister might have better understood Helena's intentions, but he'd relinquished control. The imp only understood the purpose of the firearms, and the intentions of the men wielding them. It knew of only one purpose for alcohol.

Later, Helena would have time to reflect and be amazed at the renewed clarity and the strength instilled in her at seeing her husband and son in danger on the street below. For the rest of her life, she would look back and marvel at how she'd shoved the heavy dresser sideways, destroying the brass doorknob, and escaped the room at a run. She'd reminisce about the look of shock on the bartender's face as she'd vaulted over the bar.

She'd snatched a bottle of 90-proof whiskey and a fresh-lit oil lamp from one of the tables before racing out the batwing doors.

It was this second item that she hurled at Hollister once he'd turned his back.

Truman watched as silent blue flames engulfed the outlaw's torso. The gunman bellowed and spun around like a bucking bull, trying to throw off whatever was tormenting it. Then the lumbering man changed directions and headed straight toward Isaac. The boy stumbled back, and for one heart-stopping moment, Truman felt sure that, even on fire, Hollister would gun down his son.

The outlaw took another step. One foot gave out with a crack and he collapsed.

Truman rose to his knees for a better angle. He saw Bad Hand in his jar near the outlaw's outstretched broken ankle. Something black and viscous oozed from the burning man's mouth. Helena sat in the dust opposite him some twenty feet away.

Isaac bolted and fell into his mother's embrace. A vinegar-dipped stone seemed to have lodged in Truman's throat, and his vision blurred with tears.

"Truman!" *Truman!*

Dual warnings came to his ears and mind, and Truman looked around the street. Bullock hurried up from his left. Bad Hand looked on from his perpendicular view in the jar at the outlaw's feet. Truman turned to stare again at the black goop. This was the imp, he knew, in its weakened form. But this time there was no one he could rely on, no one to whom he could defer. Preacher Smith was dead, so, perhaps, was Shen Liu. And Makohloka had returned to his tribe.

Truman sprang to his feet. He raced toward Helena. Her eyes widened, and she rose to meet him. Truman nearly knocked his wife down as he wrapped his arms around her in a fervent embrace. He kissed her lips, pouring as much love as he could into the action. Then, not daring to risk waiting another moment, he stooped and retrieved the empty whiskey bottle.

The perverse imp had crept, slug-like, into the shadow cast by the Franklin Hotel, perhaps seeking refuge in the darkness under the boardwalk.

Ignoring the pain from his bullet wound, Truman Bonner knelt and scooped the imp into his improvised glass prison. He shook the bottle until the obsidian glob plopped to the bottom, where it immediately began its slow but determined ascent.

Truman looked at his wife, trembling as the adrenaline left his body. "Did you happen to bring along a cork for this?"

Helena, now holding Isaac close, only tilted her head back and laughed.

CHAPTER 11

TIE A KNOT IN THE DEVIL'S TAIL

"I STILL DON'T UNDERSTAND why we had to roll him over," Truman said.

"Because I refuse to shoot a man in the back," Sheriff Bullock said.

Truman didn't think the outlaw would have survived his burn injuries for long, but he said nothing more on the subject.

Hollister, they had decided, would be buried in a pine box. The imp needed something more substantial.

Three figures now stood two hundred feet inside the confines of a natural cavern near Deadwood.

"Isaac, set the bottle there on that ledge," Truman said. Isaac did as instructed and then stepped back. "Now, we dump the gunpowder we hauled in here and go back the way we came. Isaac, unravel this fuse and I'll light it at the mouth of the cavern. We'll bury this source of evil so deep that no one will ever find it."

"We have enough gunpowder to bring the whole damned mountain down on it," Sheriff Bullock remarked.

Truman itched to be away from the bottled imp. "Then let's get to it."

The ground shook beneath their feet. Smoke and grit belched out of the cavern's entrance. The horses they'd ridden tossed their heads and pranced nervously. And then it was finished.

Truman and Helena embraced. Isaac stepped forward. His parents opened their arms to welcome him into the circle.

"We each faced death," Truman said.

Helena touched his bandaged shoulder and scarred face. "For that, I am sorry."

"But we helped each other, gave each other strength." Truman held both wife and son in a tight embrace. Part of him never wanted to let them go.

Helena's cheeks dimpled as she smiled. "Yes, and for that, I am thankful."

Despite the hell she'd been through, Truman still found her beautiful. "I acted like a damned fool, getting up on my high horse. Will you forgive me for that?"

Helena's eyes brimmed with tears. She nodded. "Of course. Will you forgive me?"

"Isaac and I need you to stay safe. From now on, we hope you will exercise... restraint."

Helena nodded. "I will do my best. I promise."

"That's all I can ask."

"There's too much wickedness and evil in this world," Helena observed. Isaac nodded his agreement.

"But there's a lot of goodness in it, too," Truman said.

"I feel like I've woken from a nightmare, but nightmares don't leave scars." Tears finally spilled over her sunburned cheeks.

He kept his fears in check and stroked her cheek. "We'll heal together."

"Why won't Isaac talk to me?" Helena's voice shook. "And what happened to his hair?" At this, she gave in to her guilt and sorrow. Sobs wracked her frame.

Truman held her close. "That's a story for another day. Just know that he still loves you with all his heart."

When Helena quieted, she looked up at Truman, biting her lip. "Do you think that whatever got into Hollister will stay buried in the tunnel?"

Truman took a deep breath and held it. He gazed at his wife, and then at his son. He glanced at Sheriff Bullock, standing near the horses. Bullock saw him looking and touched his fingers to the brim of his hat. On the ground at his feet, Bad Hand floated in his jar, eyes closed.

"If it comes back, we'll be ready," Truman said. "After what we've been through, I bet we could tie a knot in the tail of the Devil himself and kick his ass straight back to hell."

Helena grinned and grabbed the lapels of Truman's battered oilskin duster. "I like the way you think, cowboy. From now on we work together." She planted a kiss on his lips.

"Together," Truman agreed. "Now let's go home."

The Bonners returned to their homestead on the edge of Sturgis.

They rested, healed, and tended to their chores. Helena wept bitter tears when she discovered the extent of her son's grievous injuries.

Sleepless nights reigned. Helena sipped burning liquid from a small flask she kept secreted away. Truman stayed up late, brooding and reading from his weathered Bible. And Isaac, paralyzed by night terrors, often lay awake until the night sky turned gray with the light of dawn.

Though they had vowed to work together, each chose to battle their demons alone.

Summer gave way to fall. Winds tore leaves from branches, the grasses browned, and fall soon bolted away like a startled doe. Then winter swooped in and dropped blanket after blanket of snow across the region. With the arrival of spring, the snows melted, and heavy rains followed, washing across the Black Hills and the nearby prairie.

Atop a certain hill near Deadwood, something wicked rode on those frigid fast-running waters, traveling like poison in a bloodstream until it finally sprang free.

ACKNOWLEDGMENTS

The author gratefully acknowledges the assistance of
Leslie Cline in the preparation of this collection.

*The author would also like to thank Joseph Shelton for several concepts,
phrases, and editing in Pedestrian Encounter.*

STORY NOTES

REDUCED TO TEARS. It's scary how certain practices and attitudes become normalized. This is one of a trio of stories collected here that explore the possibilities of a dystopian near future.

AMELIA. I knew all along he'd saw her arm off. I added the bonsai information later, along with a more hopeful ending, at the urging of an editor. I think I like the original better.

WISH GRANTERS. I read a speech somewhat like this one for a charity event. I kept the notes, wondering how easy it would be to twist something beautiful into something horrible. Extremely easy, as it turned out.

A PEDESTRIAN ENCOUNTER. J. Robert Shelton is a brilliant writer. He writes stories that I can't. We tried to collaborate and couldn't quite get anything to mesh. This story would not exist without him, however. Several key ideas, phrases, and line editing came from Joseph, and I thank him for his continuing friendship.

Fear Incarnate. Originally written for a themed anthology that never got off the ground. The premise is perhaps a bit too much like a certain Stephen King novel. Maybe that's why it never sold. I reworked this story several different times and couldn't bear to discard it, so here it is.

The Sodbuster and the Spider. This might be my sentimental favorite in this collection. Another weird western, this one about hero worship and rude awakenings. Again, an editor encouraged me to add a more hopeful ending prior to publication. I strongly prefer the jarring shock ending, and have separated the pages so if you wish, you can skip the happy ending.

Esoteric Insurance, Inc. Evan Dicken did all the heavy lifting on this story. It is three-fourths his, and I owe him a great deal of thanks for allowing me to reprint it here. Evan and I met online when he took first place in an online flash fiction writing contest. (I took second.) Evan remains a friend and continues his fine writing.

The Burial Shroud. I am a dreamer who wants humanity to live in peace, harmony, and equality. I don't think that's too much to hope for.

Snow Flies. This weird western is an homage to Jack London. The shrewd horse bent on self-preservation surprised me. It didn't know about his ruse until I typed it. Personal experiences led me to choose eastern Wyoming as the setting; it's treacherous in winter.

The Horla Returns. I played with several points of view while keeping the story quite short. I took the concept of the Horla, an entity created by Guy de Maupassant in the story of the same name, and placed it in the thick of the space race of the late 1960s and early 1970s.

INSOMNIA. I've always loved micro-fiction and flash fiction. Sleep deprived parents—with a depraved twist.

PETE GETS OFF THE FENCE. The original version had Lucifer running for president. Nearly every other story in this collection has aspects of horror, or ends on a depressing note, so I decided to rewrite this one. This story, and thus the end of this collection, is meant to leave readers hopeful and optimistic.

BOTTLED SPIRITS. My favorite subgenre is the weird western. This publisher was great to work with. Longtime readers will recognize two or three of these chapters as early short stories. Some aspects of this story hit close to home for me. And a lot of the story elements are true Deadwood history.

ABOUT THE AUTHOR

Adrian Ludens is the author of *Ant Farm Necropolis* and *Cobwebs: Tales of Dread and Disquiet*. These dark fiction short story collections are available online in paperback and Kindle formats.

Ludens is the program director and afternoon host on a heritage rock radio station and public address announcer for a AA hockey team. He enjoys reading and writing horror fiction, listening to all types of music, watching hockey, hiking, and exploring abandoned buildings.

He lives with his family in the Black Hills of South Dakota.